ODESSA
AGAIN

ALSO BY DANA REINHARDT

A Brief Chapter in My Impossible Life
Harmless
How to Build a House
The Things a Brother Knows
The Summer I Learned to Fly

Dana Reinhardt

ODESSA
AGAIN

Illustrated by Susan Reagan

WENDY
LAMB
BOOKS

Text copyright © 2013 by Dana Reinhardt
Jacket art and interior illustrations copyright © 2013 by Susan Reagan

All rights reserved. Published in the United States by Wendy Lamb Books, an imprint of Random House Children's Books, a division of Random House, Inc., New York.

Wendy Lamb Books and the colophon are trademarks of Random House, Inc.

Visit us on the Web! randomhouse.com/kids

Educators and librarians, for a variety of teaching tools, visit us at RHTeachersLibrarians.com

Library of Congress Cataloging-in-Publication Data
Reinhardt, Dana.
Odessa again / Dana Reinhardt. — 1st ed.
p. cm.
Summary: When nine-year-old Odessa Green-Light stomps out her frustration at being sent to her room after shoving her annoying little brother, one particularly big stomp sends Odessa flying through the floorboards and mysteriously twenty-four hours back in time.
ISBN 978-0-385-73956-6 (hardcover) — ISBN 978-0-385-90793-4 (lib. bdg.)
ISBN 978-0-375-89788-7 (ebook)
[1. Time travel—Fiction. 2. Remarriage—Fiction.] I. Title.
PZ7.R2758Od 2013
[Fic]—dc23
2012008231

The text of this book is set in 12-point Goudy Old Style.
The illustrations were rendered digitally.
Book design by Trish Parcell

Printed in the United States of America

10 9 8 7 6 5 4 3 2 1

First Edition

To Noa, who was kind enough to let me steal many of her ideas.

*And to Zoe and the rest of Johnny Galang's class at Live Oak School,
thank you for being this book's first readers.*

The New House

There comes a day in the life of every big sister when it's simply no longer suitable to share a bedroom with your toad of a little brother.

For Odessa Green-Light, that day was a Tuesday.

They'd only been living in the new house a few months. Odessa and Oliver shared a room, like they had in the old house, and like they did in Dad's apartment. This new house, of which Odessa was not particularly fond, had one redeeming feature that the old house she missed so much did not.

It had an attic.

From the first time the landlady gave them the tour— with someone else's scribbles on the kitchen wall, and someone else's stickers stuck to the dryer that had dried someone else's clothes, and the narrow wooden staircase scuffed from someone else's shoes—Odessa had her eye on that attic.

"You'll love it here," the old lady barked at Odessa, as if this were an order and not a wish.

Odessa doubted very much that she would love it there, but she did think that she might love living in the attic, a full flight of stairs removed from Oliver.

She asked, but of course her mother said no. If there was one thing Odessa could count on, it was Mom saying no to the things Odessa wanted most.

So a few months back, on move-in day, a day Mom tried to make cheery by blasting old-fashioned music and singing into a broom handle, Odessa unpacked her stuff into one half of a too-small bedroom while Oliver the Toad unpacked into the other.

And each day since, or at least every weeknight and every other weekend, which were the nights she spent at her mother's, Odessa had begged to move into that attic, but it hadn't worked.

Begging rarely did.

She'd also tried cajoling, bamboozling, and hood-winking.

"Not a chance," Mom said.

Sometimes, however, victory is found in unlikely places.

Oliver discovered the field mouse that delivered this

victory in the backyard. Oliver didn't seem to know how to get along with real live people: his terrible shyness got in the way. But there was no denying he had a way with rodents.

It was a Tuesday, which meant the next day was a Wednesday, word-study day, and Odessa had set her mind to moving into word group N, which required some studying.

The fourth-grade class was divided into word groups L, M, and N, and although Mr. Rausche chose letters from smack-dab in the middle of the alphabet, Odessa knew that as an M, she was only a second-level word-study student.

Smack-dab in the middle.

Odessa loved words. And she always tried her best to use the ones that other people too often ignored. But loving words and knowing how to spell them were two different things, and Odessa knew she would never make the move to group N without mastering the illogical rules of spelling, which was nearly impossible to do with Oliver crashing around her too-small room.

So she told him to get lost, not having any idea that this would lead him to their new backyard, where he'd find a field mouse sniffing around a chew toy that someone else's dog had left in the grass. Nor did she guess that Oliver would sing softly to this mouse until it wandered into his outstretched palm, at which point he would carry it into their bedroom and drop it down the back of Odessa's pink T-shirt with the turquoise stripes.

Well.

Odessa did what any reasonable person would do. She shrieked, ran to find her mother in the kitchen, and threatened to sue in a court of law if she couldn't move into the attic.

From her mother's lips sprang these three beautiful words:

"I. Give. Up."

And so Odessa found herself tucked in bed by 7:45 that Tuesday night under the quilt Mom pulled from one of the attic's boxes. A quilt sewn as a gift for the darling baby Oliver, who had grown up to be a pesky toad.

*

Odessa had been sleeping in the attic for exactly three nights before it happened.

24 Hours

One of the reasons Odessa did not love the new house was that she'd seen it for the first time the day after Dad told her that he was getting remarried.

To *re* something means to do it all over again, so *re-marrying* should have meant he'd be getting married to Mom again, not getting married to someone else.

But Odessa didn't say this to Dad as they sat in a booth at Pizzicato and he made his announcement. Odessa and Oliver loved Pizzicato. Dad hated it. That he'd taken them there without any begging should have been the first warning sign.

The second was when he clinked his glass with his fork and said he had *big news*.

Odessa preferred small news. Big news was never good.

She'd cried that night, and Mom had held her.

"I don't want to be de-hyphenated!" she wailed. She'd never much liked the name Green-Light. If you were a woman named Green, and you met a man named Light, wouldn't you run as fast as you could in the opposite direction? Probably. But her parents didn't. They fell in love and got married and had kids whose names they hyphenated, and then fell out of love and got divorced, and now the most important thing in the world to Odessa was to hold on to the name Green-Light.

"Nobody is taking away your hyphen," Mom said, stroking her hair. "You will always be Odessa Green-Light, for better or for worse."

That night, it definitely felt *for worse*.

The next day Mom took her to see the new house they'd be renting because they'd finally sold the old house that Dad had moved out of the year before.

So Odessa had disliked the house from day one, but now that she'd moved to the attic, that had started to change.

Oliver's behavior didn't change, however.

It started with him mimicking her ("Oliver, have you seen my pencil case?" *"Oliver, have you seen my pencil case?"*) and refusing to stop ("You're so annoying!" *"You're so annoying!"*), and it ended with the comment he made under his breath about how she *like*-liked Theo Summers, something she had only just admitted to her best friend, Sofia, that afternoon.

Sofia had called, as she always did, just after Odessa finished her snack.

Sofia had been eying Odessa and Theo since they'd all been assigned to the same hexagonal table at school.

"You *like* him," Sofia said. "I can tell by the way you stare at him."

Theo sat directly across from Odessa. Where else was she supposed to look?

"Yeah," Odessa said. "He's funny." She also thought he was smart, but she knew this wouldn't matter much to Sofia. In the world of fourth grade, funny mattered. Smart did not.

"But do you *like* him like him?"

Today Odessa had admitted that she thought he was cute, especially since he'd stopped cutting his hair, and that yes, she guessed that meant she *liked* him liked him.

This is just what Oliver mumbled to her: *"You like-like Theo Summers."*

She'd always suspected that Oliver eavesdropped on her phone calls, and now she had the proof. So she shoved him.

Hard enough to knock him off his pigeon-toed feet.

And he fell.

They were in the kitchen, clearing the dinner dishes like Mom made them do every night before dessert. Tonight it happened to be butter-brickle ice cream, Odessa's favorite.

Mom was by the sink, exactly where she'd been

standing three days earlier when she'd thrown up her hands and said, "I. Give. Up."

One of the reasons Odessa loved words was that sometimes the very same words could have a totally different meaning. So tonight when her mother shouted, "I. Give. Up," she didn't mean *You can have what you want.* This time she meant *You are in huge trouble.*

"I'm tired of the fighting!" she hollered. "To your room, Odessa. Now. TIME OUT."

Odessa could have explained what had led her to shove Oliver, but she was too angry. Too tired of being blamed for his toadiness. So she stormed out of the room yelling, "My pleasure!"

"And don't come down until I say so," her mother called after her.

Odessa stomped through the house and raced up the narrow attic steps, slamming the door behind her.

She flopped down onto her bed. *I'm almost ten years old*, she thought, even though her birthday was still half a year away.

What ten-year-old gets a time-out?

Odessa jumped up and began to pace the creaky floorboards. *Oliver is shy with other people; why can't he be shy with me? Why is he always nosing around in my business?*

She wanted to smash something. When she felt this way she'd usually reach for the oversized sock monkey Sofia had given her on her sixth birthday and bite him on the belly.

He didn't seem to mind.

They had an understanding.

But the sock monkey was downstairs in the room that was now Oliver's, because her move to the attic wasn't finished. For example, she still had no desk. No mirror. She didn't have the posters she'd torn from the pages of the tween magazines Mom didn't like her to read.

Odessa noticed just then that despite having none of the essential things, she *did* have a hand-painted pottery cupcake sitting on top of her empty bookshelf.

A cupcake that belonged to Oliver.

Mom must have brought it up by mistake. Odessa's

hand-painted pottery was shaped like an ice-cream cone. They'd made these pieces at I Did It Pottery, on a recent Saturday afternoon with Uncle Milo.

Odessa reached for the cupcake, threw it to the floor with all of her strength, and watched, with wonder, as it smashed into tiny shards.

That felt good.

But what felt even better was the sensation of those shards crunching beneath the soles of her orange Converse high-tops.

So she stomped.

And she stomped harder.

She jumped up and down on that broken cupcake, smashing the shards to dust, until finally the creaky floorboards gave way beneath her, and she fell.

Have you ever fallen?

Down some stairs? Off the jungle gym? Out of your bed in the middle of the night?

Well then, you know what was happening to Odessa: that upside-down, over-under, inside-out feeling.

She landed with a thud.

Right in the middle of her bedroom floor.

It wasn't her old bedroom floor directly below the attic. This was the *attic floor*. The very floorboards through which she'd just fallen.

Odessa gripped her stomach. Then she scratched her head. This made no sense at all.

Mom's order rang in her ears: *Don't come down until I say so.* The type of order her mother called "nonnegotiable."

Even so, Odessa took the stairs quietly. When violating a nonnegotiable order, it's best not to stomp your way down from your room.

She found Mom and Oliver sitting at the dinner table, enjoying their dessert without her, which hardly seemed fair, considering that butter-brickle ice cream was *her* favorite, and nobody else's.

"Hi, honey," Mom said, grinning.

"Hello . . . ," Odessa said carefully.

Maybe all was forgotten. Maybe she should just take her seat and not offer any explanation for why she'd come down from her room without permission.

So she sat. Right in front of a piece of carrot cake.

Carrot cake was *not* her favorite.

And it was the same dessert they'd had the night before.

Odessa didn't want to push things, but she couldn't help herself. Sometimes things, like little brothers, needed to be pushed.

She asked politely, "What about the butter-brickle ice cream?"

"We don't have any," Mom said. "But I'll get some for tomorrow night, how 'bout that?"

Again, Odessa tried out her politest voice. "Yes we do, Mother. We bought it today. Remember? It's in the freezer."

Duh. Where else do you keep ice cream?

Odessa got up and went to the kitchen. She opened the freezer to find an empty space where the butter-brickle ice cream had been.

"WHO ATE ALL THE ICE CREAM?" she shouted.

Back in the dining room Mom and Oliver stared at her funny.

"Tonight we're having carrot cake," Mom said slowly. "And tomorrow, if you can find another way of asking, I'll be happy to buy some butter-brickle ice cream. Now take a seat."

Odessa sat. "But we had this last night," she said glumly.

"No we didn't." Oliver had frosting on his lip. "We had pineapple slices."

Odessa knew that if she opened her mouth to tell Oliver that, *actually*, they had pineapple slices the night *before* last, it would come out in a way that might get her sent to the attic again. So instead she pushed her carrot cake around her plate with her fork.

"Are you feeling okay?" Mom asked.

No, Odessa wanted to say. *There's no more butter-brickle ice cream, AND I don't understand why you're not still mad at me.*

"My tummy hurts," she said.

Mom reached over and put a hand on Odessa's forehead. "Maybe you should go lie down." She tucked a strand of hair behind Odessa's ear.

As Odessa pushed back her chair and took one last look around the table, she noticed something else.

Something that gave her the same upside-down, over-under, inside-out feeling.

Mom and Oliver were wearing what they'd been wearing the night before, when they'd all eaten carrot cake, not pineapple slices, for dessert.

Odessa looked down at herself. Amazingly, she too wore yesterday's clothes, though she had no memory of changing.

She wasn't feeling well.

Not well at all.

Up in her attic Odessa threw yesterday's clothes in the hamper and put on her favorite pajamas. She crawled underneath the quilt of teddy bears and reached over to turn out her light. The last thing she saw before she closed her eyes and drifted off to sleep was this: Oliver's pottery cupcake.

Sitting on top of her empty bookshelf.

In one perfectly intact, un-stomped-upon piece.

23 Hours

Early the next morning, when Odessa's alarm clock began to tweet (she preferred the sound of birds to buzzing, beeping, and the *William Tell Overture*), she rubbed her eyes.

What a strange dream she'd been having.

Falling through floorboards. Broken pottery. Carrot cake that should have been ice cream.

Uncanny, she thought.

She got out of bed and dressed quickly. When she came down to the kitchen, Oliver was halfway through his glass of chocolate milk, and he stuck his tongue out at her from beneath a chocolate-milk mustache.

Mom slid a plate of scrambled eggs on rye toast in front of her and said, "Eat up. The clock is ticking."

This wouldn't have been odd if her mother said this

every day, the way her teacher Mr. Rausche always started each morning by saying, "Best feet forward."

But her mother had never said anything about the clock ticking, unless you counted *yesterday* morning, when she said this as she slid a plate of scrambled eggs on rye toast in front of Odessa right after Oliver stuck out his tongue from beneath a chocolate-milk mustache.

"I'm sorry to rush you, love," her mother said, "but I have a meeting. Chop-chop."

And yes, that was exactly what her mother had said the day before as Odessa reached for her fork. She said she had a "meeting," which Odessa knew meant she had a "job interview."

Mom hadn't worked in an office since Odessa was born, and Odessa preferred it that way, so she didn't much like it yesterday when she knew Mom was going off on a job interview, and she didn't like it any more today.

Odessa had already been here.

Here in this moment.

Today was yesterday. All over again.

Odessa felt dizzy. Clammy. The smell of the eggs made her want to throw up, and she might have, if it weren't for her absolute mortal fear of vomit.

She swallowed. Hard.

Eat up. The clock is ticking.

Sure, but why was it ticking backward?

At that moment, Odessa had two choices.

One: she could stand up and run around in circles, screaming and tearing at her hair.

Or two: she could shrug this off. Shake the dizziness right out of her head. Wipe the clamminess off of her palms.

She could choose to believe that she'd only dreamed this day. That she hadn't really lived it. That her dream from the night before was even more uncanny than she'd thought, because it had predicted what this next day would bring.

Odessa decided to go with option number two.

She kissed her mother good-bye out of sight of the school bus, and she climbed on board. She watched as Claire Deloitte placed her backpack on the empty seat next to her so that Odessa would have to sit someplace else. Thomas Macon folded a paper airplane and tossed it over his shoulder toward the back row, just like she knew he would, but this time Odessa ducked so that it missed hitting her between the eyes, as it had yesterday.

(Or in the dream she'd had that she was mistaking for yesterday.)

She went through the day like this. It was sort of like sleepwalking. She felt discombobulated.

She ate spaghetti and meatballs in the cafeteria again, she listened to Ms. Gomez conjugate the verb *to remember* (*recordar*), and she watched the same film about earthworms that was no more enlightening upon a second viewing.

She came home and ate a snack and went to her room and the phone rang and it was Sofia and they talked about homework and then Sofia asked if Odessa *like*-liked Theo Summers and Odessa admitted that she thought he was cute, especially since he'd stopped cutting his hair.

And of course Oliver said something about Theo Summers under his breath, proving that he'd eavesdropped on her conversation, and even though what she wanted to do more than anything in the entire world was to reach over and shove him hard enough to knock him off his pigeon-toed feet, she didn't.

She held her arms at her sides.

She went back to the table, sat down, and caught her breath, and a minute later her mother placed a bowl of butter-brickle ice cream in front of her.

She ate it.

It was her favorite, after all.

Odessa cleared her bowl and excused herself. She went upstairs to the attic, but not before grabbing a hammer from the tool drawer and slipping it under her shirt.

She got down right next to her floorboards. She pushed

them and listened as they creaked. She tried to pry one up, but couldn't. She tried another. And another.

The floor was solidly nailed down.

She put the hammer on her shelf, next to Oliver's pottery cupcake. She walked back and forth across the floorboards. She slid across them, as if she was skating on the pond near Uncle Milo's. She reached for the cupcake. She held it up over her head, but then she put it back on the shelf. She didn't have the *I need to bite my monkey on the belly* feeling. She was perplexed, not angry.

Odessa poked at the boards with her toe. She put both feet together and jumped.

Nothing.

She jumped again. And again. She closed her eyes, held her breath, and jumped as hard as she could.

And then . . . she fell.

Over-under, inside-out, upside-down.

She opened her eyes to find herself lying in bed.

Maybe I've hit my head, she thought. *And I've been in the hospital, and now I've been sent home, and everyone thinks I'm going to die, but here I am, finally, waking from my coma.*

That was the only explanation she could come up with, because she did not remember going to bed, and anyway, people in comas probably have strange dreams.

She crept downstairs in her pajamas to find her mother in the kitchen, washing dishes.

"Odessa, honey. I thought you weren't feeling well. What are you doing out of bed?"

She leaned into Mom's outstretched arms. She closed her eyes against her mother's chest and let her mother take in a few whiffs of her scalp. Typically, she didn't let her mom get away with this sort of behavior. She was in fourth grade. She wasn't a baby. Kids her age weren't supposed to allow their mothers to smell their heads.

But tonight it felt good.

Because maybe Odessa had just woken up from a coma.

"Mom?" she asked, without opening her eyes or disentangling herself.

"What, honey?"

"How long have I been asleep?"

"It can't have been more than an hour. You really should go back to bed."

Odessa could barely get out the next sentence. It caught someplace in the middle of her throat.

"What did we have for dessert tonight?"

Her mother chuckled.

"Is this about the ice cream again?" She leaned back and took Odessa's face in her hands. "I really didn't know how much you hate carrot cake. I promise that tomorrow I'll pick up some ice cream. Just for you. Deal?"

Odessa nodded, but only because she was unable to speak.

"Now, honey, I think you should go back to bed."

Odessa took the stairs slowly. Going back to bed meant sleeping only to wake up again on the same day *for the third time in a row*. She locked the attic door behind her.

20

She grabbed her journal and sat on the floor, because she still had no desk. She took out a pencil.

Despite being a group M speller, Odessa was excellent at math.

She did some quick calculations, and as she did she felt a clicking in her brain. Just like when a difficult math problem suddenly made perfect sense. She was too smart to believe there were actual cogs and wheels turning inside her head, but sometimes that was how it felt.

What caused this clicking was Odessa's memory of coming to her room the night before, between dinner and dessert. She'd come to use the upstairs bathroom, the one she liked best, and while in there she'd thought about something she wanted to write in her journal, so she darted up to the attic, sat down on the floor, and wrote the following:

If I stop caring that Claire won't talk to me anymore, she'll start talking to me again. Just like the way Oliver gives me back what I want right after I don't want it anymore.

Odessa flipped back a page in her journal and found the entry. She flipped to a fresh page and began to scribble furiously.

The first fall through the attic floorboards had taken her back exactly one day.

Twenty-four hours.

She landed on the floor of the attic because that was exactly where she'd been twenty-four hours earlier, writing about Claire in her journal.

She did some more calculations.

The second fall took place on the same day as the first. Butter-brickle ice cream day. Although she had taken it later, after dessert, because she held her arms at her sides and did not shove Oliver. And this time, her math told her, she'd landed twenty-three hours earlier.

Flabbergasting, she thought, tossing her journal and its scribbled equations across the room.

Was this it?

Was this her life?

Would she always have to relive this day?

Was she doomed to an existence of unappetizing cake made from a vegetable?

No! She wouldn't let that happen.

All she had to do was not jump. Easy enough. The clock would tick forward so long as Odessa walked lightly on her attic floor. Better yet, she could avoid the middle of her room at all costs.

Yes.

Avoid the middle.

That was exactly what Odessa Green-Light did for the next month.

22 Hours

Odessa had almost forgotten about those strange days of falling through the floor. She must have been running a fever. A high one, the kind that makes you hallucinate. Anyway, it was silly. Impossible. It didn't deserve her attention. Not another thought. She'd even thrown away her journal after picking out a new one with a hummingbird on the cover from the stationery store.

Odessa was moving forward.

Mr. Rausche had promised she could make the switch to group *N* after five consecutive perfect scores on her weekly word-study quizzes. So far Odessa had taken four, and she'd spelled each and every word correctly.

Odessa had her attic and she had privacy from Oliver, and she was starting to like the new house. The afternoon school bus route took her by her old house, and she'd see someone else's shoes on the front porch, or someone else's bike out on the lawn, or deflating balloons tied to the mailbox, and though in the first days these discoveries made her feel like she'd swallowed a brick, lately she'd just think: *Look, someone must have had a birthday.*

Jennifer, the woman Dad was remarrying, had moved into his apartment. Jennifer was different from Mom. She wasn't tall and bony with soft parts Odessa knew how to find. Jennifer was soft all over, in a nice way, and she had brown curly hair and smelled good and her lips were always shimmery and her eyelids sparkled. Odessa had met her lots of times, and she was always really friendly, and once she even let Odessa wear some of her gloss when her lips were chapped, but Jennifer was like the shoes on the porch or the bike on the lawn—she belonged to someone else's family.

Odessa preferred her time at Mom's house. She liked the Green House more than the Light House. Especially since she'd moved to the attic.

She'd begged for a rug, and even though Mom wasn't usually quick to buy her what she wanted, she'd gone out and gotten her a purple cheetah print, which brightened up the room while also hiding the floorboards.

It was a win-win.

Odessa returned Oliver's pottery cupcake and collected her ice cream cone. She took her clock and another one from the living room that nobody seemed to miss. This way, she could be doubly sure of the time.

Mom had gone on half a dozen job interviews. She'd wear a blazer with her jeans and tie her long hair up in a bun. Sometimes she'd even put on makeup. But so far, nothing seemed to work out. What luck!

Odessa and Sofia were moving up in Dreamonica, an online game world in which they'd built identical mansions and between them owned a dozen puppies. They were best friends in Dreamonica, like they were in real life, and their characters looked exactly the same, the opposite of real life. Mom allowed Odessa twenty minutes a day online, an improvement from the fifteen minutes she'd been allowed in third grade.

Odessa and Theo Summers had been moved to adjoining seats in the hexagon and assigned to each other as math buddies. Math was easy. It made sense. It was the opposite of silly or strange or inexplicable. Odessa was good at it, and what a lucky thing that she could be good at something with Theo Summers by her side.

So all was going pretty well, until another fateful Tuesday.

Tuesday meant the next day was a Wednesday, word-study day. It was to be the fifth quiz on which Odessa would get a perfect score.

But she forgot to study.

This time she couldn't blame Oliver. Or a field mouse.

Or the fact that Dad was *re*marrying. The only person to blame was herself.

This sort of thing happens, but it didn't happen often to Odessa. So when she arrived at school on Wednesday morning and Mr. Rausche said, "Best feet forward," Odessa felt a sudden chill. Sofia stared across the hexagon at her.

What's wrong?

Sofia knew how to read Odessa's face. They were best friends. They could communicate without using words.

I forgot to study!

Sofia cringed. She knew how important this quiz was to Odessa. *Oh no!*

Maybe she could have scored perfectly anyway, but she

was upset, and her fate was sealed with the pesky word *thorough*, into which Odessa inserted a *w*.

It wasn't a failure, exactly, but that's how it felt.

And anyway, *scrupulous* was a much better word than *thorough*.

She sulked for the rest of the day. Sofia reminded her that in Dreamonica it didn't matter if you knew how to spell *thorough*, you could still live in a mansion, but that didn't help much.

On the bus ride home, Odessa almost sat on Claire's backpack, just to see what she'd do about it. She almost tapped her on the head and said, "Hey? What gives? We were friends last year, not best friends, but friends. Now you won't even talk to me." But of course she didn't. She chose a seat alone and stared out the window. When the bus passed her old house, she cursed the new owners for not cutting the roses before they died on the vine.

Odessa couldn't even be cheered up by butter-brickle ice cream.

She stared at the dish in front of her as Oliver inhaled his while babbling on about recess handball.

She took a taste.

It reminded her of something.

Not of the ice cream parlor where she discovered that butter brickle was her favorite, where Dad first allowed her a cone in place of a cup. Unlike Mom, he didn't care if ice cream wound up on her dress.

27

No, this taste reminded her of something else.

Of those strange days when she fell through the floorboards and sat down not once, but twice to a piece of carrot cake. Those days when she figured she must have been struck by a terrible fever, because nothing about them made any sense.

Those days when she must have been hallucinating.

But . . . what if she hadn't been?

What if she really did fall through the floor? What if she really *could* go back? If she'd gone back twenty-four and then twenty-three hours, the next time she'd go back twenty-two. She could live this day again and study for the test and get her fifth consecutive perfect score, so that she could move up to group N.

What if?

That night, when Odessa went to bed under Oliver's old baby quilt, she had a dreamless sleep, the kind from which you wake up full of energy. Just what you need when you set your alarm for four a.m.

Tweet. Tweet. Tweet.

How she loved the sound of birds.

She didn't love waking up early, but she needed time to go over those words, to remember that there is no *w* in *thorough*. And she wanted to make certain there weren't any other words on her list that sounded as though they should contain letters they did not.

She wanted to be *scrupulous*.

She turned off the alarm. The ink-black sky gave her

nothing to see by. She stumbled to her desk, the one her mother had finally moved up to the attic, with Uncle Milo's help. She flipped on her lamp and looked at her calendar with the cats on it.

She removed Wednesday's picture of two Siamese kittens wrestling in a flower bed to reveal a fat Calico reaching for a ball of string. He was Thursday's cat, and it was Thursday. More specifically, it was Thursday at a little past four in the morning, one day after Odessa had failed to get a fifth consecutive perfect score on her word-study quiz.

She threw Wednesday's kittens in the trash and stepped into the center of her purple cheetah-print rug. She'd been walking around it for a month now, avoiding the floor underneath. It felt soft and inviting between her toes.

She tapped her foot lightly.

She got down onto her hands and knees and pushed at the boards beneath the rug, listening to them creak. She stroked the cheetah print with her fingers.

Odessa loved this rug, and wouldn't it be a terrible thing if she jumped through the floorboards and lost it? If the rug became stuck someplace between today and yesterday? Trapped in the *betwixt*?

Her attic would look so dull without it.

But worse, what if *she* got caught in the *betwixt*? What if *she* never made it back to yesterday? How would it feel to never see her family again? Mom? Dad? Uncle Milo?

Odessa was a reader, and she'd read books about kids

opening doors or climbing through wardrobes into other worlds, and though she loved these books, she didn't think she'd like to live in any world other than her own. She wanted to live with her own family, even if that family lived in separate places, and even if that family included Oliver.

She rolled up the rug and stashed it out of the way. Then she walked back into the center of the attic, quickly, before her fears could get the better of her, and she closed her eyes, held her breath, and jumped.

The next thing Odessa knew, she was lying in her bed.

She opened one eye and looked at her alarm clock.

6:07

She opened the other and looked with both eyes at the clock she'd taken from the living room.

6:07

From her dormer window she spied the first light of day—orange and pink and blue blended together like a watercolor painting.

She'd made it! It worked!

It was almost one full hour before she usually woke up. Far too early to start the day—unless it was a Wednesday, with a word-study quiz to prepare for.

Odessa climbed out of bed and kept to the edges of her room, avoiding the center of the floor. She raced over to her desk and stared at the picture of a long-haired white cat asleep on top of a washing machine.

Tuesday's cat.

This made no sense at all. How could it be Tuesday? It was supposed to be Wednesday.

Word-study day.

But then Odessa understood. It was 6:07, after all, so it took a moment to remember that she always removed yesterday's calendar page first thing when she woke up.

It was time to remove Tuesday's cat, because it was Wednesday morning.

She ripped the long-haired white cat from the pad, and there they were: two Siamese kittens wrestling in a flower bed.

It was twenty-two hours earlier.

Wednesday morning at seven minutes past six.

Odessa sat down at her desk with her word list and quizzed herself.

Over and over and over again, until it was time for breakfast.

Downstairs, Mom gave her cinnamon toast again (luckily, Odessa loved cinnamon toast), and she climbed aboard the bus and watched Claire block the seat next to her with her backpack. She arrived at school, where Mr. Rausche said, "Best feet forward." Sofia didn't have to read her face. She wasn't panicked. She took her quiz and aced it.

There is no *w* in *thorough*.

That afternoon she was sent home with a new packet of words to study.

She was now a proud member of group N.

Odessa Green-Light was no longer smack-dab in the middle.

21 Hours . . . 20 Hours . . .
19 Hours . . . 18 Hours . . .
17 Hours . . .

Imagine everything you'd do over if given the chance.

That thing you said at lunch that made everybody laugh because it was stupid?

Forgotten.

The humiliating *thwack* of the dodgeball against your thigh and the red mark it left behind?

Erased.

The misunderstanding that sent you to the "take a break" chair, when you weren't really talking during social studies, you were only asking Jeffrey Mandel to return your pencil?

Over.

These are the sorts of things that sent Odessa back to the center of her attic floor, the rug rolled up and stashed near the bookcase. She would shut her eyes tight, hold her breath, and jump.

She jumped to undo something about her day that had gone a way she didn't like.

What power.

How easy.

Still, there were choices to make.

What needed undoing?

And was undoing it worth living the whole day over again? Worth using up another jump back in time?

What about the things she would have to endure for a second time just to change the one thing she wanted to undo?

Take the farting incident.

Odessa knew that a loud fart could be a good thing *if you happened to be a boy.*

If you happened to be a girl, farting was a whole different story. It was something to be avoided at all costs. Something to live in mortal fear of. But living in mortal fear of something doesn't mean it won't happen to you.

Like vomiting. Odessa feared vomiting, but sometimes she'd get the stomach flu. Usually right after Oliver got it, because in addition to being a toad, Oliver was a walking germ-fest. Odessa feared shots. But she got them. She was afraid of thunder, but that didn't keep storms from coming.

Odessa feared farting.

In front of other people.

Especially farting in front of somebody who looked cute since he'd stopped cutting his hair. Somebody she *like*-liked.

But still, it happened in front of Theo Summers.

During math.

Multiplication tables, to be precise.

Theo looked at her and she looked away, but she could feel how hot her face was. She didn't need a mirror to know she'd turned scarlet. Lobster-colored. This happened when she got embarrassed, and it was why her mother sometimes called her Odessa Red-Light. Like getting stuck with the hyphenated *Green-Light* wasn't annoying enough—even her own mother teased her about it. Her own mother, who along with her father had *de*-hyphenated the whole family.

Odessa waited for Theo to make some joke to Bryce Bratton. But he didn't. And because of this, because he quickly looked down at the math problems on the hexagonal table between them, Odessa's *like*-like blossomed into full-blown love.

But Theo knew.

He had heard.

And he'd never forget.

This left Odessa with no choice but to go home and jump through the floor.

Still, there were parts of this day she didn't want to relive.

On the day of the farting incident, Odessa had a checkup after school at which she received not one, but three shots. And that night there was a terrible thunderstorm. The window-shaking kind. The kind that made her rethink wanting to sleep in a room alone.

But neither shots nor thunderstorms seemed very big at all when stacked up next to the horror of Theo Summers hearing her fart.

So that night, as the thunder rattled her bones and the lightning lit the darkening sky outside her window, Odessa rolled up her cheetah-print rug.

They'd just finished dessert. Chocolate banana pudding wasn't her favorite, but it was a close second. When she considered living through the shots and the thunder again, she thought: *At least there'll be pudding!*

Odessa tapped her toe on the exposed floorboards.

The thunder crackled outside. Terrifying. A sound like the whole world splitting in two. It reminded Odessa of the time she and Oliver dropped a watermelon out their bedroom window onto the back patio just to see what would happen.

What happened was that Mom got really mad.

Hurry! Jump. Get away from the thunder. Wake up again, start the day fresh, and avoid that terrible Odessa Red-Light moment.

But going back seventeen hours was different from leaving something behind.

The shots and the thunderstorm were still in front of her because . . . tomorrow wasn't really tomorrow.

Once she jumped, tomorrow would become today all over again.

16 Hours

Things might have continued this way, with Odessa correcting all of her awkward, embarrassing, unfortunate moments. The pesky happenstances that are a part of any fourth grader's life.

Things might have continued like this but for one simple fact: Odessa Green-Light was a curious girl.

The type who sought to understand why certain things were so. It was this part of her that hated spelling and its nonsensical rules.

So Odessa went in search of answers.

She wished more than anything that Claire was still speaking to her. They were friends last year when they were both in Room 22. They weren't best friends, but Claire was fun, and curious. She was logical and clear-headed too. Back in third grade they'd read a whole series of mysteries about a boy named Benedict, and Claire had always solved the mystery *before* Benedict did. She didn't have to cheat and skip to the end to see how it all turned out, like Odessa.

But now Claire put her backpack on the seat next to her on the bus, the seat that used to be Odessa's, and they weren't in the same class this year. Odessa was in Room 28 with Sofia, which was nice, but not necessary, because Sofia was her best friend no matter what classroom they were in.

If Claire had still been speaking to her she might have been able to think three steps ahead like she had with the Benedict books and help Odessa find some answers about the attic floor. But no. Odessa was going to have to figure this out on her own.

Like she often did when things perplexed her, she opened up her hummingbird journal. She wrote down the things she understood, underlining them for emphasis.

Time is running out.

Each time she jumped she lost one hour, one chance.

There are only twenty-four chances.

Twenty-four opportunities to redo something, and now, with only sixteen opportunities left, she started to wonder: Had she frittered away the first eight?

I've been stupid.

She had no regrets about the farting incident, but the "take a break" chair? The red mark of the dodgeball and its *thwack?*

What a waste.

She began to understand the need to hoard her remaining opportunities.

Sixteen left. Sixteen!

She made a final note in her journal:

Don't be impulsive. Make it matter. THINK!

*

Weeks went by.

The air grew colder. The leaves went from green to red to brown before abandoning the trees altogether. The sky outside Odessa's dormer window turned black before dinnertime.

Dad and Jennifer were planning a spring wedding. Odessa's every other weekend with them was spent tasting cake and looking at flowers and trying on dresses. Odessa finally picked out a lavender one with spaghetti straps, which meant Oliver would have to wear a lavender tie, and she was looking forward to seeing that. He never wore anything but T-shirts and cutoff sweatpants.

Jennifer brought home samples of music for the reception. She'd play it full blast in the house and practice her dance moves. Dad would smile and shake his head. Jennifer knew how to make Dad laugh, which was good because sometimes Dad could be too serious. Sometimes Odessa would even dance with her.

All the wedding preparation reminded Odessa of when she and Sofia used to play princesses. Neither of them really wanted to be princesses—who could stand itchy clothes and perfect posture all the time?—but it was still loads of fun to pretend.

The only thing Odessa looked forward to with winter's arrival was the freezing of the pond near Uncle Milo's, where he took her ice-skating on Saturday afternoons. He took Oliver too, because Odessa never seemed to get to do anything, or go anyplace, without Oliver the Toad.

On a particularly gloomy Saturday, Uncle Milo, Odessa, and Oliver went to check out the pond, skates in the trunk, hot cocoa in the thermos, but it hadn't frozen over completely yet. Big shards of ice floated haphazardly, like pieces of a puzzle that would never fit together.

Oliver thought he spied a rabbit and went bounding off after it, maybe thinking he could coax it into his hands like that field mouse, and Odessa took the rare opportunity afforded by this moment alone with Uncle Milo to ask him some questions.

Uncle Milo was her mother's younger brother. Once he'd told Odessa a story about how when they were kids Mom had convinced him to do a trust fall backward so she could catch him. He closed his eyes, crossed his arms, and fell backward, but then she stepped out of the way and he cracked his head open on the kitchen floor. Odessa thought this was pretty funny in the way things are funny when they're the opposite of what you expect. She couldn't picture her mother letting her brother fall on his head, because Mom was the one who always told Odessa how she needed to show Oliver more *kindness*.

And she certainly couldn't picture Milo as a toad.

Uncle Milo was her favorite.

"Uncle Milo?" she asked. "Has anything ever happened to you that you don't really understand? I mean, like, something that makes *no sense*?"

"Of course, O." He smiled. Odessa loved his smile. And she loved when he called her O, except sometimes he called Oliver O too, and that she didn't like one little bit. "All the time. Most things in life don't make any real sense. That's what keeps us on our toes."

Odessa thought of Milo as someone with all the answers, but there were things even he couldn't figure out, which was surprising. And a little bit comforting too.

"Cool," Odessa said, though she was far from satisfied.

He squinted at her. "Are you okay?"

"I'm great."

"I know things haven't been easy. . . ."

"I said I'm great."

"I know you did. And I said I know things haven't been easy."

Odessa bit the inside of her cheek. She thought about that lavender dress hanging in plastic in the closet at Dad's. About Claire's backpack on the bus seat. About Mom's job interviews. About the word *like* and its different, confusing meanings.

"Uncle Milo, I . . ."

Just then Oliver came racing back, waving something in his hand. It was too small to be a rabbit. *It better not be another field mouse*, Odessa thought.

As he grew closer, he shoved the object into his pocket. When he reached them, he bent over to catch his breath, hands on knees, cheeks bright red with cold. Odessa resisted the temptation to call him Oliver Red-Light.

"You are never gonna"—*gasp*—"guess what I"—*gasp*—"just found."

Oliver was rarely right about things, but he was right about this.

Odessa would never have guessed.

Not if she'd had one hundred guesses.

He stuck his hand back into his pocket and took something out slowly, grabbing it by both ends and pulling it tight. He held it up proudly.

A one-hundred-dollar bill.

"Would you look at that. . . ." Milo slapped Oliver on the back. "It's your lucky day, O. You are one lucky little man."

Immediately, Odessa thought of her piggy bank and its twenty-seven dollars and eighty-three cents. She'd felt good about her savings. She'd saved six dollars and twenty-two cents more than Oliver.

She couldn't bear to do the math. She didn't want to know by exactly how many dollars and cents Oliver's savings now outnumbered hers.

Plus, there were so many things she wanted to buy. So much she could do with one hundred dollars. There were things a fourth grader needed that a second grader did not.

It wasn't fair.

"Where did you find it?" Odessa asked.

Oliver lifted his thumb over his shoulder and pointed behind him. He was still trying to catch his breath.

"Over there."

"Over *where?*" she asked. "Over where . . . *precisely?*"

Odessa had never stolen anything in her life. Sofia stole lip glosses from her older sister, and Odessa had told her it was wrong, but Sofia had just laughed and dug her pinkie deeper into the one that smelled like mango.

Now, as Odessa's plan began to take shape, she worried that she was about to do something kind of . . . wrong.

But how could it be stealing if she wasn't planning to take something *away from* Oliver? What if she was planning to get to that one-hundred-dollar bill *before* he did? Before he even knew there was a one-hundred-dollar bill to find?

"Over by that big boulder," Oliver said. "The one underneath that Christmas-y tree."

Uncle Milo laughed. He put both hands on Odessa's shoulders and squeezed. "You're not going to find another hundred-dollar bill, no matter how hard you look. It doesn't happen like that. Luck was on your brother's side today. Maybe tomorrow it'll be on yours."

Uncle Milo didn't know everything. He'd even said so himself. He didn't know that Odessa didn't need any luck.

She looked at her watch. All she needed was for Uncle Milo to take her home. Back to the magical attic that belonged only to her.

15 Hours

Money can't solve all your problems. This is something Odessa had heard adults say for most of her life. They also said that money doesn't grow on trees, but they were wrong about that, because Odessa now had one hundred dollars from beneath a tree in the woods. Uncle Milo had given her a high five when she'd found it, and Oliver had stared at her in disbelief and with a familiar envy. She felt a little guilty about going back and getting to the money before Oliver, but only a little. She was rich. That helped with her guilt, though it didn't help her figure out what was happening in the attic, because . . . money can't solve all your problems.

She continued her investigation by taking out mysteries from the library. Not the babyish Benedict ones any

third grader could solve. She went looking for *real* mysteries. There were so many of them, so many books with spines of every width and color. Maybe reading some might help her solve her own.

Sofia was not pleased.

They'd both started the series about the girl who moves to a new town and has to make new friends at her new school, but then there's this mean girl who will stop at nothing to destroy the new girl, and Odessa and Sofia were on book five when Odessa returned it unfinished at library time and checked out four mysteries.

That was one of the cool things about being in the fourth grade. You could check out four books at once. Second graders like Oliver could only check out two, but it hardly mattered, because Oliver wasn't much of a reader.

"Those look boring," Sofia said. "We don't read mysteries. Or books about fairies. And we don't like graphic novels."

Sofia had added this last category, Odessa knew, because that was the kind of book Claire read on the bus in the mornings.

"Yeah, I know. But I guess I'm just in the mood for something new."

Sofia sighed and rolled her eyes. She started to say something about how Odessa wasn't allowed to drop their series for a new one, but then Mr. Bogdasarian, the librarian, rang the bell that meant they were all to line up quickly and quietly. He timed them, and although Odessa always raced to her spot in line tight-lipped, she wasn't sure why she did. There never seemed to be any sort of prize for speediness.

When Sofia sighed and rolled her eyes, Odessa thought again, for the millionth time, about confiding in Sofia about the attic. About the loophole she'd found in time.

But something always stopped her.

Maybe it was that she knew how it would sound coming out of her mouth. *Impossible. Absurd.* And Sofia had a way of looking at Odessa when she didn't believe or understand or agree with what Odessa was saying—a sharp look Odessa could feel in the softest part of her center. She didn't like that feeling at all.

Or maybe it was that Odessa didn't believe Sofia could

help her solve her mystery. Help her understand the *why*.

It wasn't as if Sofia wasn't smart.

Sofia was in the level N word-study group too, which might have had something to do with how desperately Odessa had wanted to move up from the middle.

Sofia's math buddy, however, was Chester Spaulding, and everyone knew Chester wasn't as good at math as Theo Summers.

Anyway, Sofia didn't have much of an imagination, or Claire's detective skills, and she definitely didn't know about Odessa's house and its history.

For that Odessa turned to Mrs. Grisham, their landlady, who lived next door in a house that looked almost the same except it was pink. Odessa used to love pink, but she'd outgrown it, and now she wondered if when she got really old, she might love pink again.

Odessa hadn't seen much of Mrs. Grisham since they'd moved in, and she felt uneasy about just walking up to her front door and ringing her bell. Old people made her nervous. She didn't have any grandparents and she'd never had an older teacher, so she hadn't spent any time around old people.

Odessa picked up the newspaper that was sitting on Mrs. Grisham's front porch and tucked it under her arm. It took a very long time for Mrs. Grisham to answer the doorbell.

Odessa stood there, rehearsing what she'd say when

Mrs. Grisham finally made it to the door, but all she managed to blurt out was "Here's your paper."

Mrs. Grisham looked at Odessa the way Oliver looked at the various creatures he'd find in the backyard.

"It was sitting on your porch," Odessa added. "I didn't want anyone to take it."

"Has there been a rash of newspaper thefts in the neighborhood I don't know about?" Mrs. Grisham asked.

"Um, no. I just . . . I'm Odessa," she added, because she wasn't sure what else to say.

"I know who you are. You live in my house."

"Yes, I do."

"You didn't look too happy about living there."

"It's fine now," Odessa said. "I live in the attic."

Mrs. Grisham looked her up and down and then turned and went back inside. She didn't slam the door exactly, but she did close it rather abruptly.

The next afternoon Odessa noticed the paper on the porch again, and again she delivered it to Mrs. Grisham.

This time their exchange lasted longer.

Things continued this way. Most afternoons Odessa would pick up the paper from the porch and ring Mrs. Grisham's bell.

"Why are you always talking to that old lady?" Oliver asked. "She's weird."

"You're weird," Odessa snapped back. She gave him a shove in the direction of their house, as if she were urging

51

him home rather than just enjoying the pure pleasure she got from shoving him.

Odessa had never noticed Mrs. Grisham's paper on her porch before, but one thing was certain: since that first day she'd delivered it, Mrs. Grisham never seemed to go out and get the paper herself.

During their afternoons Odessa tried out all of her theories about the house.

She asked if magicians had built it.

"No," Mrs. Grisham answered.

Odessa asked if it had been struck by lightning.

"Nope," Mrs. Grisham said.

Odessa asked if, to the best of her knowledge, ghosts had ever been known to haunt her house.

"Not to the best of my knowledge," Mrs. Grisham sighed. She seemed to be growing tired of Odessa's line of questioning. "Look, don't worry about the house and just enjoy living there. Sometimes houses, like people, are peculiar. And sometimes they come along at just the right time. Now stop asking me so many questions. Do you want a cookie?"

Of course Odessa wanted a cookie.

So Mrs. Grisham started feeding Odessa homemade treats on her visits, and they sat in her front parlor, where she kept her enormous collection of owl figurines, and Odessa stopped asking questions. Instead she mostly talked about school, sometimes exaggerating details to make her stories more interesting.

And then, one afternoon, when Odessa rang the bell with the paper tucked under her arm, Mrs. Grisham took even longer to get to the door than she had on that first afternoon. She opened it only halfway. She wore a long floral thing with buttons that must have been a bathrobe.

A housecoat? A dressing gown?

Odessa wasn't sure what it was called, but she knew that even old women didn't go out in public in something that looked like that.

Mrs. Grisham managed a weak smile as she took hold of her paper.

"Thank you, dear."

It was the first time she'd ever called Odessa anything.

Mrs. Grisham started to close the door, without stepping outside for one of their chats and without offering any treats. Odessa grabbed the handle.

"Um, are you okay?"

"Yes. I'm fine. Just a little . . . oh, shall we say . . . *blue*."

Odessa loved the word *blue*. It said so much more than *sad* or *unhappy*. It was a word you could see. A word that painted a picture.

Odessa wasn't used to grown-ups telling her how they felt, unless they were feeling *fed up* or *out of patience*.

"Why are you blue?" she asked.

"Well, it's my birthday."

Her birthday? Birthdays were the happiest days of the year. Birthdays were the opposite of blue.

"So why aren't you . . . *jovial?*"

"Jovial?"

"You know, happy."

Mrs. Grisham smiled, and that made Odessa feel a little jovial herself.

"Oh, I suppose because when you get older, birthdays aren't all clowns and carousels and cotton candy."

Odessa thought Mrs. Grisham was closer to describing a carnival than a birthday, but still, she appreciated all those hard-*c* words strung together one after the other.

"Didn't you get any good presents?" Odessa asked.

Mrs. Grisham turned the newspaper over in her hands. "You brought me this," she said. "That's something."

"It's not much of a present. I mean a *real* birthday gift, with paper and ribbons and everything."

"I've never been much for presents," she said. "Mr.

Grisham used to give me a bunch of orange dahlias every year on my birthday. That was the best."

"Dolleeyas?"

"Yes, dahlias. My favorite flowers."

Odessa was about to ask what happened to Mr. Grisham and his dolleeyas, but then she stopped herself. She used *logic*, like Benedict. Mrs. Grisham was *blue*. She didn't have any dolleeyas. Therefore, there was no more Mr. Grisham.

"I have to go." Odessa turned and started to run.

"Thanks for the paper," Mrs. Grisham called.

"Happy birthday!" Odessa shouted over her shoulder as she raced home. She lived right next door, but still, she ran as fast as she could.

She found her mother in the kitchen, grating cheese.

"What's for dessert tonight?" Odessa asked, breathless.

"Please don't run in the house."

"Dessert," Odessa barked. "What is it?"

Her mother stared at her. "Melon," she said, drawing out the word.

"Water?"

"Are you thirsty, honey? What's going on?"

"No, I mean is it *water*melon?"

Her mother shook her head. "Cantaloupe."

Cantaloupe was *definitely* not worth sticking around for.

Odessa grabbed a fistful of grated cheese and shoved it in her mouth, dropping bright orange shreds of it on the kitchen floor.

"Odessa!"

Odessa knew grabbing cheese by the fistful would make her mother *fed up*, but she also knew it didn't much matter. She was already gone, running upstairs to the attic.

When she woke again, after the jump, it was 1:27 a.m. She pulled her comforter up to her chin, and she smiled because she had five more hours of sleep ahead of her.

Odessa loved sleep.

In the morning she ate her breakfast, and before she went out the door to catch the bus she handed her mother a note.

Odessa knew that sometimes she had better luck getting her mother to pay attention when she wrote down what it was she wanted to say. It hadn't worked with her move to the attic, but it had worked with other things.

She also knew it helped to use the word *please* as many times as possible.

Dear Mom,

Please can you buy a bunch of orange dolleeyas? And please put them outside Mrs. Grisham's front door. And please ring the doorbell so she knows to come to the door. But please don't stay around so she knows you left them.

Sincerely,
Your daughter, Odessa

P.S. Please!

When Odessa left for school that day, a day she had lived most of already, she felt the opposite of blue.

It was Mrs. Grisham's birthday, and she would find orange flowers on her doorstep. Her favorite. She'd have no idea who left them there, because she'd have no idea that she'd told Odessa how much she loved them. Maybe this would frighten her. Maybe she'd think it was the ghost of her husband. Or maybe she'd just gather them up in her arms and take a big whiff of them and shrug, knowing that there are some things in this world that don't make sense.

When Odessa delivered the newspaper that afternoon, it took Mrs. Grisham no time at all to come to the door. She opened it wide and grinned broadly. She didn't wear a long floral thing with buttons that must have been a bathrobe.

She wore a pretty red dress and shiny shoes.

14 Hours

Sofia was right. The mysteries *were* boring. And they didn't do anything to help Odessa understand what was happening in the attic.

Mrs. Grisham had told her to stop worrying, and Mrs. Grisham was an old person, so Odessa figured she must give good advice, because why else would you bother getting old?

That was just what Odessa was trying to do: she was trying to stop worrying and just enjoy the attic's strange powers.

She returned the boring, useless mysteries to the library and went back to the series about the new girl at school. There was no mystery as to how things would turn out for her—things always turned out just fine for this type of character, and given the twists and turns in her own life lately, Odessa liked this sort of predictability.

She also checked out a graphic novel, thinking that maybe if she held it in her hand as she boarded the morning bus, Claire would offer Odessa the seat next to her.

Odessa had given up pretending she didn't care that Claire had stopped speaking to her. That wasn't working. And anyway, she *did* care.

She and Claire hadn't known each other forever like Odessa and Sofia, but they'd become friends last year in third grade and Odessa didn't understand what had happened since. At first she thought it was just that they didn't have the same teacher anymore, but then the backpack started showing up on Odessa's bus seat.

Claire didn't seem to have had any real friends before Odessa came along. She was skinny and knobby-kneed, and too eager to agree with whatever was said. It's hard to pinpoint why some kids are targets for the cruelty of others, but there was no denying that Claire Deloitte was a big, fat bull's-eye.

"Claire, did you see that movie about the aardvark and the pelican that opened this weekend? Everyone's talking about it," one of the girls might say at recess.

"Yeah," Claire would answer. "It was funny."

"Ha! Ha! Ha! There is no movie about an aardvark and a pelican!"

Or:

"Claire, don't you love that song 'Dream Detectives'?"

This song Claire had to know was real; it played anytime a radio switched on.

"Yeah. It's awesome."

"Oh my God! That song is sooooo stupid. It's, like, the stupidest song *ever*."

Or this:

"Claire, when's your birthday?"

"It's on Oct—"

"Who cares!"

Maybe it was just because Odessa didn't pull any of these cruel jokes on Claire that Claire had attached herself to Odessa by the third week of third grade.

When it was Odessa's turn to stay in at recess to wipe down the desks, Claire would stay and help. If Odessa chose quiet reading time over working on the geography puzzle, Claire would read alongside her. Once Odessa opted to skip out on the birthday cake brought in by Sienna. Carrot cake. Yuck. Claire declined her piece too.

At first Odessa wondered about Claire.

Why didn't she stand up for herself? Why was she such a follower? But she stopped wondering, because she liked to be with Claire. Claire was smart. And she was funny. And despite the fact that she preferred books with cartoons, she too was a lover of words.

Now Claire spent most of her time at school with Maya, and that made Odessa feel *jovial* for Claire, because she didn't want her to be friendless.

So Odessa got on the morning bus with the graphic novel in her hands. She'd stayed up too late reading it cover to cover, and she was surprised by how much she'd enjoyed it.

She displayed the front of it as she approached Claire, who rested her arm on the dreaded backpack. Odessa took the seat in front of her.

As the doors closed with a *whoosh* and the bus lurched forward, Odessa turned around. She held the book out. "Have you read this?"

Claire glanced at the cover and then down at her lap. She nodded.

"Did you like it?"

Claire didn't respond. She probably thought Odessa was trying to catch her in a trap—asking for an opinion only so she could mock it.

"Well I read it last night and I thought it was awesome," Odessa said. "I totally didn't get why anyone bothered with graphic novels, like I thought they were going to be Calvin and Hobbes or Garfield or something, you know, baby stuff, but this book was really, really good."

Claire shrugged.

The bus stopped to pick up Mick McGinnis, and when it started up again, Odessa fell forward in her seat and dropped the book. As the bus climbed up the hill, the book slid back into Claire's row.

Claire picked it up, and for a moment Odessa thought she might shove it into her own bag or maybe toss it over

her shoulder or out the window, but she held it out to Odessa.

"If you liked this one," Claire said, "you should try *The Windchaser*."

Odessa took her book back, feeling encouraged. Bold. "Would you mind putting your backpack on the floor so I can sit next to you?"

"No switching seats once the bus is moving," Claire shot back.

She pointed to the rules posted at the front of the bus. Right above *No Chewing Gum* and below *No Shouting* it said *Pick Your Seat and Stay There*.

Claire knew Odessa followed rules. It was something they had in common. But Odessa was obviously desperate. Desperate enough to switch seats on a moving bus.

"C'mon," Odessa whispered.

Claire shook her head no. She reached for her backpack and started digging around. Odessa knew this meant: *Don't talk to me.*

Odessa could feel opportunity slipping through her fingers.

"Listen, Claire," she blurted out. "I don't know why we aren't friends this year, but maybe if you just told me what I did, then I could apologize."

Claire looked at her. "What would be the point? You'd just say 'I'm sorry,' but you wouldn't really mean it. Apologies don't mean anything when you make someone apologize." She shrugged. "That's what my mom says."

Odessa's mother said this too. Their mothers must have read the same book about raising children. Mom never made her apologize to Oliver. Instead she'd make her ask, "What can I do to make you feel better?"

She tried this out on Claire.

Claire just sighed.

"I guess you could make me feel better by knowing what you did in the first place. But since that isn't going to happen, I'll just tell you, and then you can give me a fake apology and go back to hanging out with your real friends and leave me alone."

Odessa's stomach did a flip. Something like the upside-down, over-under feeling she got when falling. Odessa's stomach flipped because it was one step ahead of her brain.

She suddenly knew what Claire was going to say.

This was about that afternoon last summer when she and Sofia ran into Claire at the mall.

She asked what they were doing, and Odessa said they were going to see a movie, and Claire asked which one, and Sofia drew her finger across her throat behind Claire's back, letting Odessa know: *Do NOT invite Claire.*

Odessa's mom walked over and said hi to Claire and asked what she was up to. Odessa said that Claire was busy and couldn't come to the movie with them, even though Claire had said nothing of the sort.

Claire walked away fast, almost running, saying she

had to go meet her babysitter at the food court, and there was something about the way she almost-ran that made Odessa sad for Claire, but then she and Sofia went to see the movie, and it was really funny because this humongous dog talked with this New York accent and Odessa managed to block out the whole thing until just now, sitting on the morning bus.

Or did she really block it out?

If Odessa had really forgotten about that day, then why did she remember it so clearly right now?

Claire began to tell Odessa about that afternoon at the mall. How happy she was to see Odessa, because they hadn't seen each other since school got out.

Odessa was listening to Claire but at the same time she was cursing her attic floorboards. Why did it have to be a matter of hours? Why couldn't she go back months? If she could return to that day last summer, she'd have ignored Sofia's silent warning and asked Claire if she wanted to come to the movie, which she was hearing now from Claire would have been impossible anyway, because Claire had to be at her sister's play.

But of course that wasn't the point.

"I'm really sorry," Odessa said. "And you aren't making me say anything. I'm saying I'm sorry myself."

Claire sighed. "I wish that were true."

Odessa turned and faced forward. Her eyes stung with tears. She'd tried to be a good friend to Claire, and she'd tried to be a good best friend to Sofia. But she'd done everything wrong.

She shoved the graphic novel into her backpack. How stupid to think that a book could fix things. The book was not the answer. The answer had been right there in front of her all along.

Odessa couldn't go back to the summer. But she could go back to this morning. She could leave the book at home and she could get on the bus with a letter in her hand.

It was easier to get people to pay attention when you wrote down what it was you wanted to say.

Odessa would do what she should have done months ago. She'd write a letter of apology, and she'd write it before Claire ever brought it up.

Odessa wrote the best letter she'd ever written. It took her three whole drafts.

Claire took it and shoved it in her bag without looking at Odessa.

But that afternoon, when Odessa got on the bus, Claire's backpack was on the floor, the seat next to her empty.

Odessa sat with Claire and rode the bus home.

13 Hours . . . 12 Hours . . .

Odessa had to admit that there were benefits to moving from a house you loved so your father could remarry someone who was not your mother, and the main benefit was that you got to have two Christmases.

At Mom's, Uncle Milo cooked breakfast while Odessa drew with her new artist's pencils and Oliver played with his new hamster.

Oliver had always wanted a hamster. He'd begged, cajoled, and bamboozled, but her parents had said no, because parents know that hamsters smell foul.

But now that the decision was Mom's alone, Odessa knew she'd given Oliver what he wanted more than anything, just like she'd given Odessa the attic she'd wanted more than anything, because there were other things

Mom couldn't give them, like a Christmas in their old house with their father.

And also, Oliver was lonely.

Odessa had wanted her own room, but Oliver had not. He pestered Odessa and mimicked her and eavesdropped on her, but he hadn't wanted her to move out. He didn't want to sleep alone. Getting the hamster meant he wouldn't have to.

Milo suggested Oliver name him Mud, so that when people asked, Oliver could say, "His name is Mud." They all thought this was funny, even if Odessa wasn't sure why.

They went to Dad's apartment Christmas night. Dad and Jennifer had set up a tree twice as big as the one at Mom's and covered in fake snow. Odessa used to beg for a tree with fake snow, but her dad said they were "cheesy." Now Dad had one, and Odessa didn't know if he'd gotten it for her, or if Jennifer liked the trees with fake snow too.

There were other things Odessa and Jennifer both liked. They both liked radio 101.3, which played songs Mom called *insipid*. They liked sparkling lemonade, which

Dad kept stocked in the fridge. They liked to do crosswords, and sometimes they'd work together on one from a book Jennifer had bought of not-too-easy/not-too-hard puzzles.

That night there was a fire in the fireplace where the bulging stockings hung.

Uh-oh.

Normally, melted chocolate is one of the world's greatest inventions, but on Christmas night at Dad's the chocolate he'd put in their stockings melted all over the other things in there, like the animal erasers and the headbands and the tween magazines Mom didn't like Odessa to read.

They all laughed about it, and anyway, there were more presents under the tree with the fake snow.

Oliver got a new Star Wars Lego set, and Odessa received a new dictionary.

"Jennifer picked this out for you," Dad said, giving her a look. Odessa knew the look meant: *Give Jennifer a hug.*

Odessa looked away. "Thanks, Jennifer." She wasn't in a mood to hug Jennifer. Then she added, "I love it," because this might make Dad happy, and also, it was true.

Odessa opened the dictionary and inhaled its new-book smell. It was a grown-up dictionary with tiny print and no glossy photos. As she flipped through the pages, she saw that they were filled with purple marks.

"I hope you don't mind that I went through it," Jennifer

said. "I highlighted some of the unusual words I thought you might want to learn. It should help with the crosswords and Scrabble too."

Odessa had to admit, even though she didn't want to hug her, and even though she didn't want it to be true, that Jennifer had given her the best of all her Christmas gifts.

*

By the end of vacation Odessa was ready for school to start. She was tired of staying indoors. Tired of Oliver. Tired, even, of playing Dreamonica, in which she and Sofia now had more puppies and bigger mansions with swimming pools and waterslides and their characters were big TV stars. She was ready to leave the online world for the real world, but mostly, she was ready for recess.

Theo had been teaching her how to shoot baskets, and she wasn't half bad, but then Bryce Bratton had started saying they were in *looooove,* so her lessons had come to an abrupt stop right before vacation.

Maybe over the break Theo would have blocked out Bryce, the way she'd blocked out that day at the mall with Claire, and they could start shooting baskets again. That was what she hoped when she went back to school that first day.

Odessa the Optimist.

But then Theo showed up with a new buzz cut and everything went downhill.

Odessa still thought he looked cute, because love means not caring if someone's hair is shaggy or bristly. Love means caring about what's on the inside and not on the top of someone's head.

So she was fine with the change.

She was *not* fine with what Sofia did.

During morning math Sofia sidled up to their side of the hexagon and said, "Oh my God, Theo, I can't believe you shaved off all your hair. Odessa liked it shaggy."

Ouch.

When Odessa had told Sofia she thought Theo Summers was cute since he'd stopped cutting his hair, she'd trusted Sofia not to tell anybody. Especially not Theo! That's what it means to have a best friend, whether in the real world or in Dreamonica. Your secrets are supposed to be safe.

What Sofia had done was no different from asking Odessa to trust her, and then stepping out of the way and letting her fall and split her head open on the kitchen floor.

After school Odessa went straight to her room and cried the tears she'd been holding in since morning math. She liked to imagine a place inside her, a place like that water tower not too far from the pond where she went skating, a big tank that could store all her bad feelings until she was somewhere safe enough to unlock that place and let everything out.

When she was done sobbing on her bed, she was still

angry and wasn't sure what to do about it. Sometimes shoving helped. Or throwing things. Also stomping.

What a terrible mistake.

And it was only the first of two terrible mistakes.

What she had was precious, she knew this, only thirteen opportunities left, and she knew to take great care with precious things. But she was just so angry, so *fed up*, that she'd gone and stomped on her attic floor without thinking about the consequences.

Mistake number one.

The next thing she knew it was thirteen hours earlier, and she was going to have to relive a day she wanted to forget.

It wasn't something she could undo, because it hadn't been her doing in the first place. And even if she could avoid it by knocking the hexagon over as Sofia approached or creating some other diversion, it wasn't going to take away the fact that Sofia had said it, that she had stood by and let Odessa fall back and split her head open on the floor.

Odessa decided, as she tossed and turned in her bed in the wee hours of a morning she'd already lived through, to be mature about it. To confront her troubles. To take Mom's advice and talk about her feelings rather than going around stomping and shoving. She would catch Sofia at school, before the first bell, and ask her nicely not to say anything about Theo's hair.

That was what she did.

Sofia wrinkled her nose. "Why would I say anything about Theo's hair?"

"Just don't. Okay?"

They were standing on the steps to school and right at that moment a bus pulled up. Theo climbed off with his new buzz cut, and Sofia's jaw dropped.

"How did you know?" she asked.

Mistake number two.

"Odessa! Have you guys been talking on the phone? Have you been emailing? Did you see him over vacation? Is something going on with you guys and you aren't telling me about it? Are you like *boyfriend-girlfriend* now? Geez! I thought we told each other everything."

She turned and ran up the stairs. Odessa watched her go while Theo, with his new buzz cut, walked right past her without saying a word.

Odessa thought about walking away from school, from math, from recess, from Sofia.

She might have if she'd had anyplace to walk to, but home was too far and she wasn't allowed to cross many of the streets on the way.

The first bell began to ring.

She'd never been late to class. She hadn't been late yesterday, because she hadn't talked to Sofia out on the steps. She didn't bother running. Late was late.

The fourth-grade rooms were on the second floor, but

the second-grade rooms were on the first, right by the stairwell, and as she approached Oliver's room she was surprised to find him sitting out in the hall, his face in Red-Light mode.

"Oliver?"

The hall was for the bad kids, the ones the teachers couldn't handle. Oliver was pesky, he was annoying, he was shy, but he wasn't *bad*.

"Go away," he said. "Please. Go away."

She recognized his *I'm about to cry* look, and because Odessa knew she'd do anything to avoid crying at school, she left him sitting there.

Without her asking questions, maybe Oliver could fill up his inner storage tank and hold it together until he got home and could be alone in his room.

Odessa tried to remember how he seemed after school on the yesterday that was now today. She couldn't remember. She couldn't, she realized, because she never bothered with how Oliver was feeling, especially yesterday, when she was so fed up. She'd sat next to Claire on the bus like she did every day now. She didn't notice where Oliver sat, because she never paid any attention to Oliver. But this afternoon she sat next to him. Luckily, Claire didn't seem to mind.

"What are you doing?" he asked.

"Sitting with you."

"Why?"

"Can't I sit with my brother if I want?"

"You never sit with me."

"I am today."

He turned and stared out the window.

"Why were you out in the hall?" Odessa asked.

He shrugged.

"Did you get in trouble?" Stupid question. Kids don't sit out in the hall just to breathe the fresh air.

"It wasn't my fault."

In Odessa's experience, most things were Oliver's fault, but this wasn't the time to say so.

"Whose fault was it?"

"Blake Canter is always picking on me, but I'm the one who gets in trouble."

Poor Oliver.

It was one thing to be the kid who got picked on. It was another thing entirely to be the boy who got picked on by a *girl* half his size.

"What happened?"

Oliver bit the nail on his thumb. That was what he did when he was upset or scared. He'd been doing it since he'd given up sucking it, at the mortifying age of seven.

"She took my hamster. Stole it from my backpack. She was waving it around and showing everyone and calling me a freak, and when I tried grabbing him back from her, Ms. Farnsworth told me since I can't keep my hands to myself I should go sit in the hallway."

"You took Mud to school?"

"Of course not. I took Barry."

Barry was the stuffed hamster Oliver had been sleeping with since forever.

"Why did you even take Barry to school?"

Oliver shrugged. "I don't have any friends."

She wanted to tell him that he wasn't helping matters by taking a worn-out stuffed hamster he refused to let Mom put in the laundry to school, that what he needed to do was be less shy and quiet, but she knew the damage was done. Once you're known as the boy who needs his stuffed hamster, it's a reputation that tends to stick.

Odessa leaned back in the bus seat and sighed. This day had been only a little bit better than this day had been before, and yet she knew she had no choice but to go back and live it all over again.

She thought about the randomness of things. Today had been a big mistake. It was her mistake number one. And yet . . . if she hadn't mistakenly fallen through the floorboards and had that fight with Sofia on the steps, she wouldn't have been late and she wouldn't have ever known that Oliver was having a day that was probably even worse than hers.

*

On the third take of this not-so-great day, Odessa snuck into Oliver's room while he was in the bathroom brushing his teeth, took Barry, and hid him at the bottom of Oliver's hamper.

On the bus she sat with Claire. Oliver was chewing his thumbnail. Odessa wanted to tell him that today would be a better day than it would have been had he found Barry, but she didn't. She didn't tell him for the same reason she waited for Theo to get off the bus before she asked Sofia, nicely, not to mention his hair.

If Odessa had learned anything from her adventures in the attic, it was to never make the same mistake twice.

11 Hours

It was another morning, with another one of her mother's "meetings," which meant that her mother was rushing Odessa to finish her breakfast (*Chop-chop!*) and to make some sense of the mass of tangles that was her hair (*Are small animals nesting in there?*) and to pick out something more appropriate to wear (*It's February, honey, not July*).

Odessa ate quickly, and she worked her hair with a brush, but she had no intention of changing her clothes. Girls in the fourth grade wore layered tank tops.

Her mother was opening and then slamming shut every drawer in the kitchen.

"*Somebody needs her cof-feeeee,*" Odessa singsonged under her breath to Oliver, who muffled his giggle with his hand.

"Not today," her mother muttered to herself. "Of all days, dear God, not today."

"What's wrong, Mom?"

"I just can't . . ." She picked up her purse and dumped the entire contents onto the kitchen floor. "Where on earth are the keys to the van?"

Mom always lost the keys to the van. Dad used to tease her that she should wear them around her neck like a "Latchkie kid." Odessa had never heard of the Latchkies or any of their children. Then Dad explained that a Latchkie kid is actually a *latchkey kid,* which is a kid who comes home from school to an empty house and has to let herself inside, fix her own snack, and get her homework done all by herself.

Odessa didn't offer to help. She wasn't much good at finding lost things, and even if she had been, the bus would be here soon, and even if the bus wasn't coming soon, she wasn't sure how she felt about Mom going back to work.

It sounded sort of dreamy when Dad first explained it, but that was back when Odessa couldn't imagine a life without Dad at work and Mom at home. That was before he moved to his apartment and Mom moved to the new house. And now that Mom was going on job interviews, Odessa imagined coming home to an empty house and fixing herself a snack, and she didn't find it dreamy at all.

She didn't want to be a latchkey kid. The girls in fourth grade didn't wear keys around their necks.

Odessa went off to school, leaving Mom sifting through gum wrappers and receipts on the kitchen floor.

Her day was uneventful.

She came home and brought Mrs. Grisham her paper, which she hadn't done in a while. Mrs. Grisham had baked ginger cookies, and Odessa wondered how many days she'd baked cookies without anybody stopping by to share them, so she ate four, but this didn't make her feel any better.

She went home and opened the front door. (She didn't need a key; it was unlocked.) She called, "Hi, Mom."

No response.

"Mom!" she yelled up the stairs.

Nothing.

She wandered through the kitchen, panic rising, and into the living room.

Mom sat on the sofa. The TV was on.

Some lady in a white billowy pantsuit was giving all the people in the studio audience some kind of prize, and then other ladies were jumping up and down and hugging each other, and while this should have been sort of exciting, or at least interesting, Odessa couldn't concentrate on what was happening because . . . her mother was watching TV!

In the middle of the afternoon!

Rule number one in the Green House: *No TV in the daytime.*

Okay, so maybe rule number one was *No hitting or*

pushing. No TV in the daytime was definitely rule number two.

"Mom?"

Oliver was sitting next to her. He didn't care about ladies giving away prizes to other ladies, but he would have been happy to watch anything, because he loved TV.

"Hi, honey," her mother said, eyes on the screen. "Good day at school?"

"Um, yes. Good day at home?"

"Sure."

"Did you find the keys?"

"No."

"So you missed your meeting?"

"Yep."

"Mom?" Odessa reached for the remote control. "Can I turn off the TV?"

Odessa was a keep-the-TV-on type, but she clicked the power button. She sat down next to Mom.

"I'm sorry you missed your meeting."

"Oh well, I suppose it wasn't meant to be."

"What do you mean?"

Mom stretched out her legs and pulled the throw blanket up to her chin.

"I mean if the job was the right job for me, then I would have made it to the interview. I wouldn't have misplaced the keys. The Universe would have seen to it that it all worked out."

"So it's the Universe's fault?"

The Universe. Why hadn't Odessa ever thought to blame her mistakes on the Universe?

Mom laughed. She nudged Odessa with her toe.

"Maybe you should give the Universe a time-out," Odessa said. "Send the Universe to its room."

Oliver jumped up and threw his arms out wide. "You should kick the Universe in the privates!"

"Inappropriate," Mom said, trying not to laugh. Then her smile disappeared. She pulled her feet back and curled them underneath her.

"You don't need a job," Odessa said.

"Yes, honey, I do. That's just the way it is now that I'm on my own."

Odessa wanted to tell Mom that she wasn't on her own. That she had Odessa and her toad of a son and Uncle Milo. But Odessa was quiet; she felt a sting in her eyes and didn't want to cry.

Mom looked at her. Mom knew how to see the sting even when the tears hadn't come yet. She was tricky that way.

"Oh, sweetie." She reached out and brushed Odessa's cheek. "Finding work is a good thing. I *want* to go to work as much as I *need* to. I'm ready to get back into designing. I miss it. I want to do something that puts me back out into the world."

"What was the job?" Odessa asked.

Her mother sighed. "Oh, just the kind where you get paid to do what you love."

Odessa loved making pottery. She loved the color magenta, lollipops that were too big to ever finish, and the feeling of fresh-out-of-the-laundry pajamas. She loved the smell of newly mowed grass. Butter-brickle ice cream. Theo Summers.

Odessa tried to imagine someone paying her for loving all those things.

"Sounds like a pretty good job," Oliver said.

Mom tousled his hair. "Stupid Universe," she said, even though *stupid* was a word Odessa and Oliver were not allowed to use.

"Stinky Universe," Oliver said timidly. Mom smiled.

"Contemptible Universe!" Odessa cried.

Mom put one arm around each of them.

Odessa had made up her mind, but there was no hurry to go to her attic and back to this morning to fix things. It was nice to just sit here like this.

"You know what?" Mom said. "The Universe wants us to have some ice cream."

Odessa and Oliver jumped up and raced into the kitchen. Oliver went for the spoons, Odessa for the bowls.

"Mint-chip or butter brickle?" Mom called as she headed for the freezer.

What a silly question. Always butter brickle.

"Well, would you look at that," Mom said as she stood

with the freezer door open, the cold rush of air blowing her hair off her face.

"What?" Odessa and Oliver asked in unison.

"The Universe has a very strange sense of humor," Mom said as she pulled out her frozen car keys.

10 Hours

Usually when Dad came to pick up Oliver and Odessa for their Wednesday-night dinners, he'd pull into the driveway and honk. Sometimes Jennifer was with him. Odessa liked the just-Dad nights, but ever since Christmas and the dictionary with the purple underlined words, she didn't mind so much when Jennifer came along.

On the Wednesday after Odessa had gone back to find Mom's keys in the freezer so Mom could make the job interview, Dad came to the front door and rang the bell.

Odessa opened it. "Why didn't you honk?"

"Is that a way to greet your dad?" He spread his arms out wide and she stepped into them. He pulled her close.

"That's better," he whispered into her ear. He smelled like his minty tummy tablets. Odessa missed that smell.

"OLIVER," she shouted up the stairs. "LET'S GO!"

"Wait a minute!" Dad said. "Let's go inside and talk a little."

Odessa didn't like any sort of conversation that adults announced you were having before you had it. First there was the "talk" about how Mom and Dad decided it would be better to live apart, and then the "talk" about how they were going to sell the house, and of course the "talk" about Dad getting remarried.

"Can't we just go to dinner?"

Mom walked up and Dad put his arm out. It was sort of like a handshake, but a little bit like a hug.

"Come on into the kitchen," Mom said.

Odessa followed them.

"How're things?" Dad asked Mom.

"Oh, you know, pretty good," Mom answered.

There they were, walking and talking like two old friends meeting each other on the street.

Her parents could be so weird.

Oliver came downstairs and took a look at the three of them around the kitchen table. Odessa could tell he was just as confused and uncomfortable as she was.

"So your dad and I want to talk to you about some changes," Mom said.

"I know there have been so many lately," Dad added, "and I'm sorry for that, I truly am, but sometimes change is good, and change can be exciting, and in this case you should be proud of your mother for getting a really great job."

And proud of *me*! Odessa wanted to yell. *I'm the one who found her keys.*

"You got a job?" Oliver asked, shocked, like it had never occurred to him that one of her "meetings" might lead to that.

"Yes, honey, I did. At JK Design Studio. I'm going back to interior designing. I'll be doing some landscaping work too."

"That's great, Mom." Odessa tried her best to sound excited.

"Yes, it's great, but it means we have to make some new arrangements. I'll be out of the house more than I'd like."

I'd like you to be out of the house not at all.

Odessa didn't say this out loud. She sat there fingering her necklace with the peace sign, imagining how a key might feel hanging from her neck on a shiny new chain.

"I've talked to Mrs. Grisham next door," Mom continued. "She's agreed to watch you on the days you don't have after-school activities."

"The landlady?" Oliver asked.

"Do you know another Mrs. Grisham who lives next door?" Odessa snapped. Oliver's face fell.

"She used to be a teacher, so she can be of some help with your homework."

If Mom couldn't be home, at least it would be Mrs. Grisham and not some stranger greeting her after school. Mrs. Grisham was her friend, even if she was old.

"And you can always call me at work if you need anything at all," Dad added.

Odessa looked at her father. What she wanted to say was: *Why are you even here?* But she knew it might come out sounding mean, so she searched for better words.

"Why are you even here?" she asked, because sometimes only certain words work.

Dad cleared his throat and exchanged a look with Mom. "Because in spite of all the changes, we're still a family."

If we're still a family, why are you remarrying Jennifer?

Odessa didn't say this out loud.

Instead she grabbed her coat and went to dinner with Dad and Oliver, just the three of them, and afterward Dad pulled into the driveway and honked. Mom came to the front door.

They waved at each other and smiled as Oliver and Odessa walked into the house.

Odessa thought about that smile upstairs in her room. The way her parents almost hugged. How proud Dad seemed of Mom for getting that job at JK Design Studio.

She sat down and opened her new dictionary. When the world confounded her, words brought her peace. She read some of the words Jennifer had underlined in purple.

She liked the ones that meant something other than what you'd think.

Gumshoe: a detective. NOT a person who has gum on his shoes.

And she liked the ones with meanings that matched the way they sounded.

Enigma: something that is not easily explained or understood.

*

Mrs. Grisham started watching them the following Monday. Odessa and Oliver arrived home to the smell of something delicious that turned out to be made of something not delicious at all. Zucchini bread.

Odessa knew few things with the sort of certainty that she knew zucchini does not belong in an after-school snack.

Oliver took one look at it and went straight to his room.

Odessa and Mrs. Grisham sat in the living room and talked, and it felt like those afternoons at Mrs. Grisham's house, except that they weren't surrounded by owl figurines, but by photographs of a family that didn't include Dad.

Later that week, the snack was pumpkin muffins. An improvement for sure, but still missing the mark.

Odessa ate a muffin and polished off a glass of cold milk. Mrs. Grisham asked about her day, and she said it was fine. It was easier than telling her she saw Sadie Howell talking to Theo Summers at recess and that this wasn't good at all because everyone knew that Sadie, with her pale blue eyes, was the prettiest girl in the whole fourth grade.

Mrs. Grisham was a friend, but Odessa didn't need to tell her *everything*.

On her way upstairs to call Sofia, which she still did despite the "Odessa liked it shaggy" comment, she paused outside Oliver's door. She could hear him talking quietly on the phone. Didn't he know that she used the phone every day after snack?

She put her ear to his door. Even though she hated when he eavesdropped, she had to listen.

Who was he speaking to?

He'd said he had no friends, but this couldn't be true. Everyone has some kind of a friend, even shy kids like Oliver.

"It's okay," he was saying. "You're going to be okay. I know you feel bad, but I'm here. I'll help."

Odessa creaked open the door.

"Oliver?"

He sat on the floor with his back to her, holding something in his lap.

"It's Mud," Oliver said. "He's really sick."

Odessa sat down next him and watched as he stroked his hamster. His best friend.

"His heart is beating really fast and his breathing sounds weird."

"Maybe you need to take him to the vet. Let's go tell Mrs. Grisham."

"No," Oliver blurted out. "No way."

Odessa looked at him.

"Remember Truman?" he asked.

Truman was their old cat. Mom had him since before she'd met Dad. They'd taken him to the vet one day because he wasn't eating his kitty food, and he never came home again. Oliver was barely old enough to remember Truman, but he'd since been terrified of vets. And people doctors too.

"But maybe the vet can help him." Odessa touched Mud gently.

Oliver shook his head no as a tear made its way down his cheek. Usually Oliver's tears irritated Odessa. He knew how to cry at just the right time, in just the right way, so that he always looked like an innocent victim.

Poor Oliver, she thought.

Usually when someone said, *"Poor Oliver,"* it was immediately followed by *"You're older, Odessa. You should know better."*

But today she really felt those words: *Poor Oliver.* The realness of that tear made Odessa want to help him.

"Wait here." Odessa went into Mom's medicine cabinet and took out the grape-flavored chewable Motrin. Mom gave it to her in the middle of the night when she woke up with the feeling like her knees were on fire, or sometimes her ankles, and occasionally her feet. The doctor called these "growing pains," but Odessa was never any taller in the morning.

She also took chewable grape Motrin when she had a fever or her teeth hurt and that time she'd stepped on a bee when she'd gone outside in bare feet right after Mom had said, "Put some shoes on, you could step on a bee!"

Odessa knew Mom's medicine cabinet was off-limits. She knew never to take any medicine all by herself, without adult supervision—that was why medicine came in bottles most adults had trouble opening. But chewable grape Motrin came in a box, and anyway, giving it to a hamster was different from taking it herself.

Odessa held the purple pill in her hand. She braced for the feeling of Mud's nose and whiskers on her palm, but he had no interest in her offering.

"Maybe we should crush it up and put it in his food," Odessa suggested.

Oliver shook his head. "He's not eating."

When Truman needed medicine Mom would pry his mouth open, shove the pill down his throat, and hold his jaws closed until he swallowed it.

She looked at the pill and at Mud's mouth. The pill was almost half the size of his little face. She couldn't see how this could possibly work.

"Maybe put it into his water," Oliver said.

Odessa nodded. Sometimes, not often, but sometimes, he did have brilliant ideas.

Oliver crushed the pill into the top of Mud's water

bottle and gave it a good shake, then put it back on the side of the cage. He placed Mud in a patch of sawdust just under the small metal spout.

He sniffed it.

His whiskers twitched.

He sniffed it again.

Then Mud stuck out his tongue—so little and pink—and started to drink. Odessa couldn't believe how small his tongue was. And his teeth! No bigger than grains of rice. She had to admit, he was sort of cute as he stood on his hind legs and held on to the drinking spout with his tiny little paws.

Oliver breathed a sigh of relief as a third of the purplish water slowly drained from the bottle.

He looked at his sister. "Thanks," he said.

Odessa smiled.

She went up to her attic, her chest swelling with pride. It felt good to help someone, even if that someone was a rodent who belonged to a toad.

She called Sofia, but Sofia's mom said she was doing homework and that they could talk about Dreamonica later. Odessa didn't say: *I need to talk about Sadie and why she's all over Theo, not my fake mansion with the waterslide!*

She sat at her desk and pulled out her folder. Perplexors: math problems disguised as word problems. They made her brain hurt. She put those back and took out her word-study sheet. The quiz, as always, was on Wednesday. Tomorrow. She looked over her list.

neighbor
brought
tongue
height
weird
believe

And her favorite: **misspell.**

It was nice to know that Mr. Rausche had a sense of humor.

Odessa stretched her legs and caught the cord of her desk lamp with her sneaker, pulling the plug clear out of its socket and plunging her room into almost-blackness. That was one thing about living in the attic that Odessa did not love—her small window didn't let in much light.

She grabbed her pen that was also a flashlight and crawled underneath her desk. Her father had given her this penlight. It said Clark Funds on it. She'd always wondered why Dad had given her Mr. Funds's pen, but now she was glad he did, because she'd have had a hard time finding the socket without it.

Just as she went to put the plug in, Odessa spied a little door. Well, maybe it wasn't a door, because it had no handle, but it was a small square-framed space, just big enough for somebody to crawl through.

She shined the light of Mr. Funds's pen on it.

How peculiar, Odessa thought.

She reached over to give the door a shove, and just as she did, she heard a bloodcurdling scream come from beneath her.

"Nooooooooooooooooooooooooooooooo!"

Odessa scrambled out from under her desk and down her attic steps and threw open Oliver's door to find him lying in his bed, curled around Mud's lifeless small body.

"He's not breathing!" Oliver wailed.

Mrs. Grisham raced in. She took the hamster from Oliver and looked him over carefully. She put him up to her ear as if he were a telephone.

"Oh dear," she said.

Oliver began to sob uncontrollably.

What came tumbling into Odessa's mind just at that moment was a purple word from her new dictionary.

Slipshod.

It referred to something done in a sloppy way with poor attention to detail, and though Odessa understood it to apply mostly to the way things are built or constructed, she couldn't help but feel, at that moment, that *slipshod* might also describe her whole *feed-the-sick-hamster-some-chewable-grape-Motrin* plan.

Would it have been such a bad idea to read the label?

"It's her fault," Oliver cried. "It's all her fault."

Mrs. Grisham looked at Odessa.

"W-w-well," Odessa stammered, "I . . ."

Then she ran from the room.

*

Ten hours earlier found Odessa standing on the sidewalk waiting for the bus to school. Oliver was saying something to her, but Odessa wasn't listening. She probably didn't listen the first time he'd said it either, but she wasn't listening this time around because she was waiting for Mom's car to turn the corner.

She was going to save Mud, even though Oliver had been so quick to tattle on her. It didn't seem fair to punish a poor hamster for her brother's being a toad.

To think she'd felt guilty about that one-hundred-dollar bill! Oliver didn't deserve good luck. It was no wonder the kid had no friends. Who tattles on someone for doing what she thought was the right thing? For trying to be a decent sister?

He babbled on and Odessa put her hands over her ears. No reason to be nice to him.

Just then Mom's car came into view.

It was a new ritual since she'd started work. Odessa and Oliver walked to the bus stop, where they'd meet Ben Greenstein and his mother, who waited with the three of them until the bus arrived. Mom would leave the house right after the kids and honk and wave as she drove past on her way to work.

Odessa flailed her arms wildly. "Stop!" she yelled.

Mom pulled over.

Odessa ran to the passenger door and opened it.

She spoke without stopping to breathe. "You have to take Mud to the vet—it's really important—he's really, really sick—and Oliver is too scared after what happened to Truman to tell you—but if Mud doesn't see a doctor he's gonna die."

Odessa slammed the door, ran to the bus, and climbed on.

She sat next to Claire and smiled. It was nice having her as a bus friend. She shut her eyes and took a silent vow never to enter her mother's medicine cabinet again. Never would she bear the responsibility of taking another's life, even if that life belonged to a smelly hamster with rice-sized teeth.

She didn't talk to Oliver once all day.

Walking home from the bus stop that afternoon, Odessa thought about how she could get Oliver to repay her. He owed her big-time. The problem was, he didn't know he owed her. He didn't know she'd gone back and helped him. No matter. She'd figure out a way to make him pay.

When they walked through the front door, Odessa did not smell pumpkin muffins. And she did not find Mrs. Grisham waiting for them in the kitchen.

Mom sat at the table with a serious look on her face. A face that said: *We need to talk.*

"It's Mud." Mom held out her arms to Oliver. "He isn't going to make it. I took him to the vet, but there's nothing they can do to save him."

9 Hours

Odessa had started to see herself as someone with limitless capabilities. Kind of all-powerful.

Odessa Almighty.

No more.

As it turns out, going back in time can't fix everything. Mud's demise made that clear.

Now she was just *Odessa Who Can Go Back and Correct Mistakes, Sometimes*—a title that didn't have quite the same ring to it.

She told herself that she had never killed the hamster in the first place. Just believing, briefly, that she *had* caused Mud's death . . . it didn't fit with how she saw herself.

She was a giver, not a taker.

A fixer! Not a breaker.

And now that she knew Mud was going to die anyway, she felt . . . well, better.

Oliver, however, was not recovering speedily. He rarely smiled, and had no energy to be his pesky self.

Mom offered to get him a new hamster, but he refused.

"How about a guinea pig? They're hardy!"

"No thanks."

"I'd consider a ferret."

Oliver shook his head.

"You know, we could always go back to being a cat family."

He didn't even bother to respond.

"Hey," Odessa said. "Remember when your bike got stolen and then Dad went out and got you a new one and it was way better than the one you used to have?"

Oliver looked at her. For a minute she thought he might tell her to *shut up* or ask why she had to be such a *stupid butt-brain*, but he just walked off and closed himself in his room.

Odessa listened outside his door. Was he crying? Talking to his stuffed hamster, Barry? She heard nothing.

This silence was maybe the worst sound of all.

She thought of giving him the hundred-dollar bill. Maybe that would cheer him up. But she decided against it: money can't buy happiness. At least, that was what grown-ups said.

Oliver was particularly glum over the weekend. Because they shared a room in what was now Dad *and* Jennifer's apartment, it was hard not to notice the depths of his *blueness*.

She didn't know how to cheer him up, but that didn't stop her from trying. One attempt, a happy dance, ended with her twisting an ankle.

He wouldn't play Scrabble. Jennifer had picked up a deluxe version, the kind where the board spins to face the next player, and Odessa brought along her new grown-up dictionary with the purple underlined words, but Oliver shook his head. "No thanks."

Odessa set up a runway for a fashion show, and Jennifer let her borrow her heels. She wore her lavender dress

even though the wedding was months away, but Oliver refused to put on his suit with the matching tie.

Jennifer tried too. She suggested a Lego challenge: Who can build the tallest structure in three minutes? Oliver took a pass.

And then on Saturday morning, while they were watching TV, the only activity Oliver would engage in, his favorite commercial came on. It was for a car driven by hamsters in baggy pants and gold chains, hamsters that could break-dance. Every time Oliver saw this commercial he'd laugh until he cried, except for this Saturday morning when he started crying without any laughing first.

Odessa sat across the room, stunned. She wanted to go comfort him somehow, but she took too long, and before she knew it Jennifer hurried to the couch and put an arm around the sobbing Oliver.

That was when he shouted at her.

"Don't touch me!"

Shy, timid Oliver roared like a lion.

Dad came storming into the room. "What's going on in here?"

"Nothing," Jennifer said. She stood, hands deep in her pockets. "Oliver's just upset."

Dad looked from Oliver to Jennifer and back again, and then at Odessa, as if she could do anything other than keep her heart from pounding its way right out of her chest.

The first thing she wanted to do was run upstairs to her attic. To turn back the clock and reach Oliver first. That way, if he'd shouted, he'd have shouted at her. That's the way things were supposed to be. Brothers are supposed to shout at sisters. Not at the woman your dad is going to remarry.

But Odessa couldn't run upstairs, because she was at the Light House: Dad's. Her attic was at the Green House: Mom's.

"Oliver?" Dad looked at him.

The room felt like it was shrinking. It felt like someone had turned up the thermostat.

"It's okay, Glenn," Jennifer said.

More than anything, at that moment, Odessa wished her mom was there. She'd know what to say to make the room expand, and cool down, and feel normal again.

Odessa looked at the clock above the sofa. They weren't going home until tomorrow evening, and that would be too late. She couldn't fix a thing.

Jennifer walked out of the room. Dad sat by Oliver and all at once Odessa felt that water tank inside herself filling up, not with tears, but with rage.

If Dad hadn't left their old house, if he hadn't de-hyphenated the family, they wouldn't be in this apartment, and there wouldn't be an almost-stranger named Jennifer in the other room, and Oliver wouldn't be looking so miserable because he wouldn't have screamed, and anyway he wouldn't have even been given a hamster who died, because when Dad and Mom lived together they said no to rodents.

Odessa went and took her brother by the hand. It had been so long since she'd held it. She could feel that it had grown bigger. She pulled him into their bedroom. They spent most of what was left of the weekend in there. Odessa wrote in her journal. Oliver played with his Legos.

When Dad dropped them off on Sunday evening he honked, Mom came to the door, and they smiled at each other. As Odessa walked up the steps, she thought again about their smiles and about all the things she couldn't fix.

Still 9 Hours

Odessa's tenth birthday was approaching, and she found herself wondering if this was what it meant to grow up. Did the world just get more and more mysterious? More *incomprehensible*? More *bewildering*?

There was the attic floor, of course, and then the door with no handle under her desk. There was how your best friend could step out of the way and let you split your head open, yet continue to be your best friend. There was the way two people could smile at each other, and then one could go and remarry somebody else.

She wished she could just live in Dreamonica, where she got to make every decision—how many puppies, how big a mansion, even what color hair and eyes she had.

And speaking of eyes, there was Sadie Howell, who had turned her attention to Theo Summers, big-time.

Odessa could not compete with those pale blue eyes; she couldn't even match their shade when she designed her online self.

Smile, blush, giggle. Smile, blush, giggle.

That was Sadie Howell. Hovering over Theo's desk. Sitting next to him at assemblies. Running up to him at recess.

Smile, blush, giggle.

Odessa couldn't believe this sort of thing worked. It made Sadie look kind of dumb, or—as Uncle Milo liked to say—one fry short of a Happy Meal.

But Theo seemed to fall for it. Without his shaggy hair to hide behind, Theo had no choice but to stare right back into Sadie's eyes.

All this time Odessa had thought the secret lay in math! If she could show Theo how good she was at solving equations, he'd see that she was worthy of his love.

It seemed so stupid now. Maybe Odessa's Happy Meal was the one missing the fry.

She needed a plan. Solutions to mysteries didn't fall from the sky. They didn't materialize out of thin air or show up in the bottom of a box of Honey Nut Cheerios. Library books didn't unravel mysteries, and you couldn't buy answers with a one-hundred-dollar bill. Asking the grown-ups in your life a whole bunch of questions wasn't any help either.

She needed to *do* something.

Odessa decided to start with the mystery that seemed the most solvable: the door with no handle in her attic. She needed to open that door. She needed Uncle Milo, because for one thing he was handy, and for another, if the door opened onto a secret world or an alternate universe, he was the person she'd want to take with her when she abandoned her old life for a new one.

But Milo hadn't come around in a while, and when Odessa asked Mom why, she smiled a goofy smile.

"He's been busy."

"Doing what?"

Uncle Milo was famous for doing nothing.

Mom grasped Odessa's hands and leaned in close, barely able to contain her excitement. "He's been spending time with a nice young woman named Meredith."

Meredith? *Meredith?*

Odessa immediately pictured this Meredith with pale blue eyes.

Smile. Blush. Giggle.

"He's bringing her to dinner," Mom said. "Saturday night."

Dinner was always better when Uncle Milo came over, but Uncle Milo always came alone.

Meredith? Odessa anticipated the evening with a combination of giddiness and dread.

She felt downright *griddy*.

What if Meredith didn't like children?

What if she was a sour-faced adult with no sense of humor? What if she smelled funny or had horse teeth?

Or what if she was nice and friendly and pretty like Jennifer, but still a stranger who didn't belong in the family?

Saturday morning was haircut day. It had been three months since the last visit to Snippity-Do-Dah, which only meant that Odessa's long, straight hair was a little longer and a little straighter. Oliver's short hair had grown shaggy, though not in a cute-shaggy way like Theo Summers's—more in an I-just-crawled-out-from-under-a-rock-shaggy way.

Odessa liked Snippity-Do-Dah because they gave out lollipops, and not the tiny kind you could crunch your way through in two seconds. Their lollipops lasted.

Odessa stared at herself in her mirror. She pulled long strands of hair over her face and then folded them up to just above her eyebrows, so she could see what she'd look like with bangs.

Cute.

She turned her head away and then whipped it back around to the mirror, trying to catch herself off guard. She wanted her knee-jerk reaction.

Still cute.

She picked up the phone to call Sofia. Sofia would have an opinion on bangs. She was full of opinions. She would have an opinion about bangs in general, and

about bangs on Odessa, but Odessa put the phone back down.

She didn't totally trust Sofia. And she was still a little mad at her. Sofia didn't know about the "Odessa liked it shaggy" comment, so she probably thought everything was fine between them.

But what about her reaction when she thought Odessa and Theo were hiding a secret boyfriend-girlfriend relationship? It was as if she couldn't believe Theo would ever like Odessa in that way!

Odessa had gone back and fixed all that, but still, she knew . . . even if Sofia didn't. That made it hard to trust her, though they were still best friends in real life and in Dreamonica.

It was complicated.

In the car on the way to Snippity-Do-Dah, Odessa said, "I'm getting bangs." It felt good to have made this decision without Sofia's approval.

"Oh, honey," Mom said. "Are you sure?"

"It's just bangs, Mom," Odessa shot back. Bangs were easy. Simple. Bangs were not at all complicated.

"Well, it's up to you, I suppose, but I just want to make sure you've given it some thought."

Sadie Howell had bangs. Odessa couldn't go to Snippity-Do-Dah and ask for pale blue eyes, but she could ask for bangs.

Big mistake.

When she got home Odessa rushed to her room to see what she could do about her new, not-so-fabulous look. She stared at the mirror that only an hour ago had told her bangs were a good idea. Cute, even.

Stupid mirror.

Odessa grabbed her green crushed-velvet headband. Her favorite. She wore it most days anyway, so maybe nobody would notice if she used it to hold those horrible bangs up off her forehead. But her hair just poked out and looked weird.

She had only nine falls through the floorboards left. Five fingers on one hand, four on the other. You don't need to be a math whiz to understand that nine is not a large number.

Odessa had a feeling there were important things to do with these opportunities. She wasn't sure what, exactly, but she knew she needed to make them count.

Should she use one to undo a haircut?

Probably not. After all, hair grows back.

But Odessa couldn't afford to look not-so-fabulous. There was Sadie Howell. And Meredith was coming for dinner.

Bangs mattered. Bangs were important.

*

Back at Snippity-Do-Dah, sitting in the bright yellow swivel chair, Odessa looked at herself in the mirror.

Bangs. How stupid!

"Just a little off the bottom," she said. "Thank you very much!"

8 Hours

Meredith did not have pale blue eyes or horse teeth, but she did have a good sense of humor. And she was a third-grade teacher, so she liked kids.

Odessa's third-grade teacher had been Ms. Albright. Ms. Albright was the last person in the world Odessa could imagine Uncle Milo bringing to dinner. She also couldn't imagine calling Ms. Albright by her first name, whatever that was.

She thought about the kids in Meredith's third-grade class. What did they call her? What would they think about Odessa calling her Meredith?

Odessa wore her favorite outfit—her peace T-shirt, gray skinny jeans, and pink Vans. She brushed her bangless hair until it shone.

As usual, Oliver didn't put any effort whatsoever into his appearance.

"You should change," Odessa said.

"Why?"

"Because you look like a toad in that shirt. And Meredith is coming over. And if you act like you look—that is to say, like a toad—she may decide she doesn't want to ever have children with Uncle Milo because maybe they'd get your toad genes." Geez. Oliver could be so annoying. And so clueless. "Toad," she said one more time before she slammed his door and walked away.

Odessa was glad she'd bothered with her outfit. Meredith had red hair and three piercings in each ear. She wore tall boots and a denim dress, and she looked much cooler than Ms. Albright ever did.

Meredith smiled at Milo a lot. And he smiled at her. Odessa was smiling too. It was a regular smile-fest. Except for Oliver.

Odessa felt something like guilt tug at her. Maybe she was responsible for Oliver's mood. But what could she do? He looked like a toad in that shirt. And it was her duty as his sister to tell him so.

By the time Mom brought out dessert—chocolate mousse—Odessa loved Meredith. She was deep in an *I want you to be my aunt* sort of love, and because she loved Meredith this way, she felt really bad about having to do what she was going to do next.

She needed Uncle Milo's help with the door with no handle, and she didn't know Meredith well enough yet to know what kind of company she'd be in an alternate universe, if that was where the door led. She needed to get Milo alone.

"Can you come up to my room?" Odessa asked.

"Sure, O," Milo said, and he grabbed Meredith by the hand. She had small fingers with perfectly manicured silver nails. "Let's go."

"Not her," Odessa said. "Just you."

Odessa knew how she sounded. But she couldn't think of any other way to ask, and since she couldn't come out and explain why she wanted only Milo, she was left with no choice but to come off as rude.

Uncouth.

Milo looked wounded. He turned to Meredith. She took her hand out of his and placed it on his shoulder.

"It's okay, baby." *Baby?* Meredith looked at Odessa and winked. "Sometimes a girl just needs a little alone time with her favorite uncle. I totally understand."

Odessa didn't know how to wink, so she didn't wink back.

Milo followed Odessa up the stairs while Meredith used her third-grade teacher skills to try to interest Oliver in a game of Uno.

"What's this all about?" Milo asked once they were safely in the attic. She searched his eyes for the twinkle they usually got when she and Milo were in the midst of conspiring.

No twinkle.

His eyes looked like Mom's did when Odessa left dishes in the sink, or her shoes at the bottom of the stairs.

"I need your help," she said. "I really, really need your help."

Milo softened. "Talk to me," he said.

Odessa reached for Clark Funds's penlight and shined it on the door with no handle.

Milo got down onto his knees.

"It's a crawl space," he said.

"What's that?"

It sounded fun. Like the indoor playground at the

mall Mom used to take her to when she was little, before Odessa realized that there was cool stuff you could buy at the mall.

"It's sort of like another attic. Sometimes it's used for storage."

Her attic had an attic?

"I need to get in there."

Milo narrowed his eyes. She saw just the slightest hint of a twinkle.

"I *need* to," she pleaded.

He reached over and gave it a shove. It wouldn't budge, but Odessa could have told him that.

"It's painted shut," he said. "We've just got to loosen up the edges."

He reached into the pocket of his jeans, pulled out a Swiss Army knife, and ran it along the perimeter of the small square entry. White chips of paint fell onto the floor.

Milo gave it another shove. The door shifted slightly but still wouldn't open. He worked his knife around the edges again, and this time he leaned against the door with his shoulder.

Finally, it gave way, and Milo tumbled forward, hitting his head on the wall with an alarming *whack*.

"Nothing to worry about," Milo said as he rubbed the spot just above his right eyebrow. "I don't really use my head much anyway."

Odessa hesitated. She'd visualized so many possibilities

for what lay beyond that door with no handle that she was suddenly afraid to look inside.

She wasn't afraid of finding *something.*

She was afraid of finding *nothing.*

She stared into the darkness.

"Well," Milo said. "My work is done here."

He stood up to leave. Odessa opened her mouth to ask him to wait, because what if an alternate world really did lie beyond that darkness? What if she was about to step into a new life? She'd need Milo by her side.

But she didn't say anything, because she knew what was inside that door. She knew it in her bones.

Nothing.

Milo started down the steps, but then he stopped. "You know," he said, scratching his head, "you really should try to be a little more patient with and nicer to your brother. I know it isn't always easy, but . . . he's your person in this world. And you're his. You'll need each other, all your lives."

He closed the door behind him.

Odessa sat still for a moment before grabbing Mr. Funds's light and switching it on. She didn't see the point of sitting around feeling guilty.

She held the penlight in front of her. It only lit up one small patch of darkness at a time. If Odessa were more courageous, she might have climbed inside the crawl space. Instead she sat at the edge of the opening, shining the light's small beam all around, illuminating wooden boards and cobwebs.

Just as she was about to give up and figure out how to close a door with no handle, the beam caught something.

She moved closer, holding the penlight out straight.

A small owl figurine.

Just like the ones that filled Mrs. Grisham's front parlor.

Odessa leaned in to grab it. She didn't disappear into an alternate world, but she did get her lungs full of dust. She took the owl out and wiped it off with the hem of her T-shirt. She held it and stared at its gold glass eyes.

Why was Mrs. Grisham's owl in her attic? What had she been doing up here? Did she know more than she was letting on?

Odessa placed the owl on her desk, right next to her cat-of-the-day calendar. She sat down in her swivel chair and looked at it.

Owls were supposed to be wise, weren't they? In cartoons they always had glasses and funny square graduation hats.

Please, she pleaded with the small figurine. *Help me. Solve my mysteries.*

And what she heard it say was: *Whoooo.*

Whoooo.

Whoooo do you have in this world?

She had to hand it to the owl. It was an excellent question. Who *did* she have in this world?

Dad was remarrying Jennifer. Mom had a new job. Sofia couldn't be trusted. Claire was just a bus friend. Mrs. Grisham was probably hiding something from her. Milo was falling in love with Meredith.

Oliver.

Odessa had Oliver.

Milo was right. He was her person in this world.

Odessa reached for her dictionary.

She needed the soothing power of words. She put her hand on top of it as if she were swearing on a Bible. She opened it and began to flip through the pages, slowly at first, then faster. She loved the sound of pages being flipped, the rush of air they gave off. She stopped, placing her finger randomly inside, and the word she was looking for found her. There it was, underlined in purple.

Compunction: regret; the state of feeling sorry for something.

Compunction. It was different from feeling *blue.*

She thought of Oliver and how she'd spoken to him tonight and how he'd lost the power to smile and how he had no friends other than one dead hamster and one dirty stuffed one. How she'd stolen a hundred dollars from him, robbed him of his one triumphant moment.

Compunction overwhelmed her.

When Mom came knocking at her door saying "Come down right now, young lady, you're being rude," it was a relief. A big fist had reached inside Odessa's chest and was slowly squeezing her heart and lungs tighter and tighter. She stood up, but that squeezing feeling held firm inside her.

Without stopping to think, Odessa marched to the center of her room, rolled up her cheetah-print rug, and jumped.

*

After her third visit to Snippity-Do-Dah and her third lollipop she couldn't crunch through in two seconds, Odessa brushed her hair shiny and went down to Oliver's room.

"You should change," she said.

"Why?"

"Because that shirt is too small for you and Meredith is coming for dinner. And you want to make a good impression. It's the first step toward making a new friend."

Oliver smiled at her. "Will you help me pick something out?"

"Sure," she said, and she reached over and touched his freshly cut hair.

7 Hours

Suddenly it all made sense. The reason. The purpose. After all, people don't just go falling through floorboards backward in time *willy-nilly*.

Finally, Odessa had a mission.

Project Oliver.

She would use her power to help the most powerless person she could think of. She'd make up for not having always been the world's greatest sister.

Oliver didn't know what to make of Odessa's sudden attention. He eyed her with suspicion, the way any younger brother might whose previously mean or indifferent older sister started saying things like:

"Time to lose the Power Rangers lunchbox. How about getting a Bakugan one?"

Or:

"Maybe you should take tae kwon do."

And:

"Why don't you see if that kid Jack can come over sometime? But don't call it a *playdate*, that's too babyish."

She tried not to be bossy; she knew from experience that it wouldn't help Oliver see things her way.

Everyone needs friends, especially shy kids, so Odessa decided she'd become Oliver's first friend. If he had one, others were sure to follow.

She started sitting next to him on the bus. Claire didn't seem to mind. She would turn around in her seat to talk to them, and Odessa figured it couldn't hurt Oliver's reputation to be seen with two fourth-grade girls, even if one was his sister.

A few mornings she walked Oliver to his classroom so she could give Blake Canter a look that said: *Don't mess with my little brother, even if you are littler than he is.*

After that, she wasn't sure what to do. How do you help a toad become a prince when there's no way you're ever going to kiss him?

*

Odessa showed Mrs. Grisham the owl she'd found in the crawl space. Mrs. Grisham looked up from the honey spice cake she was slicing. It was a Wednesday, a *dinner out with*

Dad day. Even if Odessa *did* want to spoil her appetite, she wasn't sure she'd do it with a honey spice cake.

"Oh, I remember that one. I haven't seen it in ages."

"That's because I found it in my attic. In the crawl space."

"Huh. I wonder how it got in there." Mrs. Grisham turned it over in her hand, and then held it out to Odessa. "Here, it's yours. Finders keepers and all that."

Odessa took it back. She'd already tried asking Mrs. Grisham all about the house and the attic, and she hadn't gotten anywhere, but she decided to try again.

"Did you ever spend time in the attic?"

"Of course. It's my house, after all."

"Did anything strange ever happen?"

"Strange things happen all the time. Now eat your cake."

Odessa took a few bites, just to be polite. Then she went upstairs and looked out her small window onto Mrs. Grisham's house next door. It looked the same, except pink. She knew from being inside that the rooms were similar, but darker and more filled up with stuff. And now she saw—it should have been obvious—that Mrs. Grisham's house also had an attic.

What if that attic had magic powers too? What if the answer to Odessa's biggest mystery lay up a narrow flight of stairs in the house next door?

Odessa waited until Saturday.

Saturday afternoon was the one time Odessa knew for sure that Mrs. Grisham left the house. She went to the farmers' market in town, where she'd buy fresh vegetables that she'd try to hide in Odessa's and Oliver's afternoon snacks. She'd buy herself a bunch of dahlias too.

When she left, Odessa walked around the outside of her house, trying all the windows and the back door. Everything was locked. Odessa had never burgled anybody's house, though she did so love the verb *burgle*.

Stupid! Of course Mrs. Grisham locked her door and all her windows. Nobody wants burglars. Especially not old ladies who live alone.

Odessa would have broken a window if she hadn't been afraid of cutting herself. She'd have kicked down the door if she had known tae kwon do.

She went back to her own house and up her attic stairs.

*

When she opened her eyes again it was 7:15 that morning. She scrambled for her bathrobe and slippers. Mom and Oliver were still asleep, so she tiptoed out of the house.

She'd never rung Mrs. Grisham's bell so early. What if old people slept late? What if she turned off her hearing aids and didn't hear the doorbell? What if she answered without any teeth?

All these questions raced through Odessa's mind as she stood on the porch, but they turned out to be all for nothing because Mrs. Grisham answered quickly, dressed and with a full set of teeth.

"What brings you here at this hour?" she asked.

"I can't find my green velvet headband. Maybe I left it over here?"

Mrs. Grisham let her in.

Odessa made a show of looking around the room, all the while waiting for Mrs. Grisham's attention to somehow get diverted.

"And you need this headband at a little past seven in the morning?" Mrs. Grisham arched an eyebrow.

"Hair emergency!"

Odessa looked underneath the sofa.

Mrs. Grisham stared.

Odessa lifted up and then replaced a pile of books on the coffee table.

Mrs. Grisham cocked her head.

Then a miracle occurred. Miracles, like answers to mysteries, don't usually fall from the sky or materialize out of thin air.

But this one did.

A teakettle whistled someplace in the back of the house.

"I'll be right back." Mrs. Grisham turned to follow the sound.

Odessa ran to the front window and undid the lock.

6 Hours

At first, breaking into Mrs. Grisham's house was exciting.

Odessa the Gumshoe.

After watching her neighbor leave for the farmers' market, Odessa went to the front porch, heart pounding. The window she'd left unlatched that morning slid right open and she crawled inside.

In the attic Odessa found boxes, musty furniture, and old-lady stuff. She shined Clark Funds's penlight all around. Nothing interesting. She cleared a space on the floorboards and jumped, over and over, as hard as she could, waiting for that over-under, inside-out, upside-down feeling.

Nothing.

When she crept back down the attic steps and out that

front parlor window, what she'd done suddenly seemed wrong. Inexcusable. It felt way worse than taking the one-hundred-dollar bill. She ran home and hid in her room and vowed she'd never burgle anyone ever again.

*

The next Monday she could hardly look Mrs. Grisham in the eye.

She'd come home on the bus alone, because Oliver had gone to Jack's house. He'd listened to her! And now he was going to play with a friend! Project Oliver was right on track.

"I have homework," Odessa said as she passed through the kitchen. She didn't even pick up one of the oatmeal cookies still cooling on the rack.

"Wait," Mrs. Grisham said. "You might need this."

She reached into her apron pocket and pulled out Clark Funds's penlight.

"You seem to have left it upstairs," Mrs. Grisham said. "In my attic."

This was a huge Odessa Red-Light moment. Maybe the worst ever.

"I . . . I . . . I . . ."

What to say? She wanted to run. Flee up to her attic and jump through the floorboards. Erase this moment. Wipe it off the map.

But she couldn't.

There was nothing she could do to prevent Mrs. Grisham from finding her penlight and figuring out that she'd violated her trust by *burgling* her house. It was too late. Too much time had passed. She didn't have enough hours left to go back that far.

"I'm sorry," Odessa said. "Really sorry. I just . . . I was just . . . I was just trying to figure something out."

"Did you?" Mrs. Grisham asked.

"Did I what?" Odessa asked.

"Figure it out?"

"No."

"And does it matter?" Mrs. Grisham asked.

Odessa thought about this. Did it matter? Did the *why* of it all *really* matter? She had to admit, now that she thought hard about it, that despite her desire to understand why and how things worked, it didn't. What mattered was the *what*. *What* she did with her power.

"I guess it doesn't," Odessa said.

"Okay then." Mrs. Grisham pointed to the cooling rack. "Cookie?"

Odessa took two.

*

Odessa developed a Grand Master Oliver Plan.

A GMOP.

It came to her while she was sitting in the principal's office. She'd never been to the principal's office, but despite all the things she'd learned this year—three-digit multiplication, world capitals, how to apply deodorant—she still hadn't figured out how to control her impulse to shove.

It was a Thursday.

PE day.

This meant that the fourth graders ate lunch earlier than usual, overlapping with the second grade in the cafeteria.

Odessa watched Oliver walk in. Before Project Oliver she would have pretended she didn't know him, but today she waved to him from across the room.

Odessa could see that his shoelaces were untied. He hadn't mastered the art of tying his own laces. How a boy could be as skilled as Oliver at building with Legos and yet so *ham-handed*, Odessa could not understand.

She stood on her chair so he could see her and she mouthed the words: *Your shoelaces.*

He looked at her with befuddlement.

This time she whisper-yelled: *"Your shoelaces!"*

In addition to not being able to tie his shoes properly, Oliver apparently could not read lips.

Odessa cupped her hands to her mouth and shouted: *"YOUR SHOELACES!"*

He heard her.

So did Blake Canter.

Rather than stopping in his tracks and bending down to tie his shoes—rather than listening to his sister—Oliver took a step forward with his tray in his hands, and when he did, Blake Canter took her little hot-pink sneaker and stood on his dangling shoelace.

Oliver's fall was *epic*.

The clatter of the dishes. The crashing of the silverware. The tray sliding ten feet across the cafeteria floor. It was a *cacophony*—but the laughter was the loudest sound of all.

It echoed off the cafeteria walls.

Oliver lay on the floor. Odessa could see that he wasn't hurt, so she ran right by him and up to tiny Blake and gave her a shove, hard enough to knock her off her hot-pink feet.

The evil little she-troll burst into tears.

And now Odessa sat face to face with Ms. Banville, the principal.

While Ms. Banville remarked on how *surprised* she was, how *puzzled* to see Odessa in her office, when Odessa had always been such a *model* student and blah, blah, blah—Odessa wasn't listening.

She was doing math in her head.

If she went straight to the attic after school she'd have time to go back and catch Oliver before lunch and tie his laces for him.

She saw no point explaining Blake Canter's trolliness.

Why bother, when Odessa would erase this visit to Ms. Banville's office, Oliver's epic wipeout, and the echoing laughter in the cafeteria?

She'd wipe it all off the map.

Odessa took stock of Ms. Banville's office. Her big swively chair, the photographs of curly-headed children, the diploma on the wall, and the big banner above her window that said FEBRUARY IS PRESIDENTS' MONTH.

This meant many things. It meant that they ate cake for George Washington's and Abraham Lincoln's birthdays. It meant a week off when some people did boring things like visit relatives, while others did awesome things like go to the Harry Potter theme park.

And it meant that someone at school got to be President for a Day.

It worked like this: they had an all-school assembly at which Ms. Banville would read a riddle, and whoever solved it first got to skip the next day of classes and sit in the principal's office acting like the principal, or the president, which meant making announcements over the loudspeaker and signing attendance slips, and—most important—it meant you were cool for one day, and usually that coolness lasted for a long time.

As Ms. Banville rattled off Odessa's various punishments—a written apology to Blake Canter, an essay on how words, not fists, are the way out of conflict, and no recess for two weeks—Odessa studied that sign.

FEBRUARY IS PRESIDENTS' MONTH.

Her GMOP started to take shape.

She would help Oliver win President for a Day! She would hand him a moment of triumph. Make up for the one she'd taken away.

Odessa had some planning to do, but for now, she needed only to go home and back six hours so that she could start this day over and tie her little brother's shoelaces in triple knots.

5 Hours

When the time came to select the President for a Day, Odessa was so excited to begin her Grand Master Oliver Plan, so proud of herself for coming up with it, that she failed to account for the problem of the shrinking of time. Since there were only five hours left, and since the assembly took place first thing in the morning, Odessa couldn't wait until she got home from school to jump through the floorboards. That wouldn't leave her enough time to give Oliver the answer to Ms. Banville's riddle.

None of this was on Odessa's mind that morning. She ate her cinnamon toast and rode with Claire to school, all the while picturing herself the hero. The one who saved her brother, who put his needs above her own. After all, Odessa wanted to win President for a Day herself. Who wouldn't? All that attention! Even better than pale blue eyes.

She was filled to the brim—to the very top of that tank inside her—with pride. She was such a good person.

Odessa the Selfless.

She arrived at school and filed into the gym along with everyone else.

She took her seat and listened as Ms. Banville said: "I'm going to read this year's riddle. Please don't shout out the answer. Raise your hand and wait to be called on." Then she leaned in close to the microphone.

Slowly, and with a fair amount of drama, she read from a slip of paper:

> *You can find me in darkness but never in light.*
> *I am present in daytime but absent at night.*
> *In the deepest of shadows, I hide in plain sight.*
> *What am I?*

A few hands shot up and then some came down just as quickly. Odessa leaned back into the bleachers. She didn't even try to solve the riddle. She didn't need to.

Ms. Banville called on a fifth grader.

"I don't know . . . maybe dreams?" she said.

"Good guess, Rochelle," Ms. Banville said. "But no, that is incorrect."

She wandered over to a kindergartner who had both

his hands in the air and was waving them so wildly they'd snagged the curls of the girl sitting next to him.

"Yes, Jeremy?"

She held the microphone to his mouth.

"Elmo?" he said.

The whole school laughed, but not the way they laughed in the lunchroom at Oliver. Or the way some girls used to laugh at Claire. They laughed because little Jeremy was adorable with his crazy hands and out-of-the-blue answer.

When do kids go from adorable to just plain weird in the eyes of everyone around them?

There were a few more guesses—*an owl, a bat, an invisible friend.* One third grader said "Big Bird" and then sulked when he didn't get a laugh.

Ms. Banville read the riddle aloud again. She scanned the bleachers.

"Theo?"

Odessa turned around and saw Theo, her Theo, with his hand in the air.

Both Theo and Odessa were good at perplexors. "If Bob eats apples but not bananas and Bertha likes pears but not oranges" and those sorts of problems. But this one was different.

Theo dropped his hand into his lap and tugged at his T-shirt. "Um, the letter *D*?" he said.

Sofia grabbed Odessa's knee and gave her a *The boy*

140

you love is about to win! squeeze. It was the perfect moment between two best friends. Nobody knew. Nobody saw. Nobody embarrassed anybody.

Ms. Banville gave a sly smile and motioned for Theo to come down from the bleachers. He stood next to her.

"How do you mean?" she asked.

"Well, there's a *d* in *darkness* but not in *light,* and there's one in *daytime* but not in *night,* and then, like, there's one in the middle of the word *shadows.* So . . ." He shrugged.

Odessa had known Theo was smart, but she hadn't known he was *brilliant.*

"Congratulations," said Ms. Banville, putting a hand on his shoulder. "Tomorrow you will be President for a Day."

Applause filled the gym, and nobody clapped harder than Odessa. She was so swept up in his victory, in his breathtaking intellect, in her sudden vision of Theo as the

President, arm in arm with Odessa, his First Lady, that she almost forgot what she had to do.

Get home. Back to the attic. She looked up at the clock. *Oh no!* She couldn't wait until after school.

Sofia looked at her. She sent a silent message: *Are you okay?*

Odessa nodded.

She thought of running home. Of all the streets she was forbidden to cross. Even if she had the courage, the house would be locked. Though she was happy she wasn't a Latchkey Kid, right now it was very inconvenient that she didn't have a key around her neck.

She needed a Plan B.

Vomit.

Her most feared thing in the world.

The fourth grade was lining up to go back to their classrooms. Sofia linked her arm through Odessa's. A cluster formed around Theo with lots of back-slapping and high-fives and all those things boys did when what they really wanted to do was hug somebody.

Theo looked happy, in his bashful way. He wasn't a bragger. He had *humility*.

Odessa felt a pang of regret. Of compunction.

Theo had won the contest fair and square. No luck, only his brilliance, which was the very core of why she loved him, long hair or short. And now she was going to snatch this victory right out of his hands.

He would never know, of course, but she hoped anyway that he'd find it in his heart to forgive her for what she was about to do.

She broke away from Sofia, ran to the front of the line, and grabbed Mr. Rausche's sleeve.

"Uuuuggghhh." She clutched her middle. "I feel like I'm going to throw up." Even saying the words made her healthy stomach turn.

Mr. Rausche looked her over, making a face. "Odessa Light-Green . . ."

Come on, Mr. Rausche, is this the time for a cheapo name joke?

She made an overly dramatic groaning noise.

"Hurry," he said. "To the nurse's office. Go."

The nurse kept her distance from Odessa as she speedily dialed her mother's cell phone.

Voice mail.

"Have a seat," she said to Odessa. "We have to wait to hear back from your mommy."

Mommy. How embarrassing. Did this nurse realize she was in the fourth grade?

"I can't wait," Odessa said. "I have to go home NOW."

"I've left a message. I'm sure she'll call back when she gets it."

"But," Odessa said, "I'm running out of time."

The nurse looked puzzled. How could Odessa make this woman understand? She had to get home so that she could jump back and give Oliver the answer.

Then . . . it came to her. Sometimes there's another

solution right under your nose, but you fail to see it because you're too focused on the obvious.

"If you can't reach my mother," Odessa said, "can you call my father?"

The nurse nodded wisely, as if this were an unusually intelligent idea. She checked Odessa's file, and dialed.

Odessa knew Dad would answer. He always had his BlackBerry within arm's reach.

The nurse hung up. "He's on his way."

Odessa's heart soared. It wasn't that she'd be able to beat the clock, it was that Dad, with all his markets and stocks and trading and his new apartment and his new almost-wife, still could make time for her. His sick kid.

Or his fake-sick kid.

When she climbed into his car, he handed her a bottle of ginger ale and one of her favorite magazines. He put on 101.3, the station she and Jennifer both loved. Odessa was in a hurry, but still, she wished the drive would last forever. She tilted her seat back a little. Dad took her hand.

Just then the next wrinkle in her plan occurred to her.

"Dad," she said. "You need to take me home."

"Where do you think I'm taking you? I'm taking you home, so you can rest up and feel better."

Odessa swallowed. "No, Dad, I mean home. To Mom's house."

Dad pulled the car over to the side of the road. He reached into his glove compartment and took out a roll of his minty tummy tablets.

144

"My apartment is your home too." He turned to face her. "I know you don't spend as much time there as you do at your mother's, but that's because of our schedules and my work, and we're just trying to make things easier for you and Oliver. That doesn't mean that you shouldn't feel like you are at home with Jennifer and me."

Why'd he have to look like he'd just lost his favorite hamster? And why'd he have to say Jennifer's name?

Odessa stared straight ahead, out the windshield of the car that wasn't moving. Even though it was her favorite station, a song she didn't like played on the radio.

"I know, Dad. It's just that I really need to go to Mom's house. The Green House. I need to go to my room. My own room. My attic room. Please. I know you don't understand, but I really need to go there. Can you take me there?"

"Your mother is at work. I don't have a key."

"Mrs. Grisham has a key. We can borrow hers."

"Wait here," Dad said. He climbed out of the car with his BlackBerry and paced up and down the sidewalk with it pressed to his ear.

"Fine," he said as he started the car engine. "I talked to your mother. I'll wait there with you until she gets home."

Odessa's feet felt heavy as she climbed the stairs to the attic. She told Dad she was just going upstairs to change into pajamas.

It was so nice to have him there. He was in his regular seat on their couch, waiting to start a movie on pay-per-

view, one of the stupid comedies they loved watching together. It felt almost normal to see him there. She could imagine all four of them together, in this new house.

She didn't miss her old house. She just missed her dad.

She looked at her clocks.

12:47

The assembly started at nine. She had some time to spare. Just enough for a movie she'd seen a billion times before.

She ran downstairs.

"What happened to your pajamas?" Dad asked.

She threw her arms around him. "Thanks, Dad," she said.

"For what?"

"For picking me up. For the ginger ale and the magazine. For leaving work early. For taking me here. For watching a movie with me."

"You don't have to thank me, sweetie. I'm your dad."

"I know, but I just feel thankful so I wanted to tell you, because if I don't I may not get the chance again and I don't want to live with *compunction*."

Dad squinted at her, then reached over and put his hand on her forehead. "Did the nurse take your temperature?"

She grabbed the blanket and put it over the both of them. She rested her head on his shoulder and they watched their movie and Odessa dozed off for a minute, and when her eyes snapped open again she thought, quickly, of two things.

One, that it wasn't strange, not strange at all, to have Dad in Mom's house. And two, that she'd better hurry upstairs or else her whole GMOP would fail.

"I've gotta go," she said, jumping up and running to the attic with the sort of energy not typically possessed by a sick child. "I'll be back," she called.

She wished that she didn't have to leave. That they could sit together until Mom got home. Mom would walk in and see Odessa and Dad on the couch, and maybe they'd smile at each other. Maybe they'd have dinner together. Maybe he could stick around until bedtime.

But she had to go back for Oliver—and there she was, filing into the gym with her class at 8:58 a.m.

The second grade had already arrived and taken their seats on the bleachers. Odessa broke from the line and ran over to her brother. She grabbed him by the collar and leaned close in to his face.

"The letter *D*," she whispered.

He tilted away from her, as if he were protecting himself from an incoming slap to the cheek. "Huh?"

"Just listen to me for once, Oliver. It's the letter *D*, okay? The letter *D*. That's the answer. I know you're shy, but you have to raise your hand and say 'The letter *D*.' That's all you have to do. I'll give you a hundred dollars if you just say 'the letter *D*.'"

She turned and ran back to join her class, taking the same seat, one row in front of Theo.

Ms. Banville started in with her instructions about not shouting out the answer, and Odessa watched Oliver. She knew that look. Pure panic spread across his face.

She glared at him. *The letter D*, she mouthed silently.

He shook his head slowly: *No*.

His shoulders slumped and he looked down at his feet, refusing to meet her gaze across the bleachers even though she sent him the strongest telepathic message she could: *Don't wimp out. Do it. Raise your hand. Don't be a toad. I wasn't planning on giving you the money, but I will, I really will, if you just do it!*

Finally, after answers of dreams and owls and bats, Ms. Banville called on Theo.

"Um, the letter *D*?" he said.

Oliver finally turned his eyes back to Odessa and shrugged.

Sorry, he mouthed.

You should be sorry, she thought. *After everything I went through for you—you blew it! I tried to help you, but you, Oliver Green-Light, are a helpless toad.*

Sofia squeezed her knee again—*The boy you love is about to win!*—and again Odessa enjoyed basking in Theo's brilliance, but she was mad at Oliver. Really mad.

Once a toad, always a toad.

On the bus home she sat next to him for what she'd decided would be the very last time.

Before she could say anything he blurted out, "I don't know how you knew the answer, but however you found out, it isn't fair. I don't want to be a cheater. And anyway," he said, his eyes welling up with tears, "I don't want to be President for a Day. Maybe you do, but I don't."

"What! You don't? What do you want, then, Oliver? Really. What do you want?" She was almost shouting at him now.

"I just want to be normal. I just want my old life back," he said, sniffling. "I just miss my old life."

A hole ripped in the water tower inside her and she could feel her anger draining from her body.

Of course. There it was.

Oliver missed his old life.

Odessa missed her old life too.

She reached into her backpack and took out her sweatshirt. She handed it to her brother so he could wipe his tears.

"Don't worry, O," she said. "I'll get you your old life back. I promise. I can fix this." Then, if only to convince herself, she added: "I have the power."

4 Hours

With Dad's wedding only a few weeks away, Odessa didn't have a lot of time to get her old life back.

But then she thought about how quickly things could change. One day Dad lived with them, the next he didn't. Mom said, "We're putting the house up for sale," and suddenly it belonged to someone else. Mrs. Grisham showed them around the new house, and the next week they were moving in.

Change can happen quickly, and Odessa just needed to be quick about it.

To *re* something means *to do it again.*

Dad needed to *re*marry Mom, not some woman named Jennifer. Just because Jennifer was nice to Odessa and had sparkly eyelids and shimmery lips didn't mean she needed to marry Dad. Odessa didn't want to hurt Jennifer, she really didn't.

Maybe when all this is over, Odessa thought, *I'll find someone nice for Jennifer to marry.*

But first things first. It was time to re-hyphenate her family.

She started with her lavender dress. It was so beautiful, so twirly and delicate. She hated to see it get ruined, but she had to do what she had to do.

It was a Saturday morning and she asked to try it on again. "It's just that I love it so much," she said.

Jennifer was in the kitchen making crepes, her specialty. They were delicious, covered in powdered sugar and chocolate. As Oliver carried his to the table, Odessa twirled right into him, slipping her hand under his plate and flattening it to her chest.

"Oliver!" she shouted.

He stared at her openmouthed.

She shot him a look: *I've got this. This is all part of my plan.* But he didn't understand. Oliver couldn't read lips, and he wasn't so great at reading looks either.

"I-didn't-do-it-it's-all-your-fault-you-knocked-into-me!" he screamed.

Jennifer grabbed a kitchen towel, but it was no use. The chocolate was everywhere. The lavender dress turned a not-very-attractive maroon.

Dad stood there with his hands on his hips.

"I'm soooooo sorry." Odessa tried to sound remorseful. "I didn't want to ruin your wedding."

"It's okay," Dad said. "We'll just have to get you a new dress."

"But it won't be this one. And I'm supposed to wear this one."

"It's just a dress, Odessa." Dad reached over and steadied his hand on the still-shaking Oliver. "And I guess this means Oliver doesn't have to wear his lavender tie."

That was Odessa's next plan, to draw on Oliver's tie in permanent marker. Now that wouldn't work either.

Okay. Think big.

It took her the rest of the weekend to work up the courage, and then, finally, on Sunday afternoon, shortly before Dad was to drive her and Oliver back to Mom's, Odessa started looking for the scissors.

If this had been the Green House she'd have known where the scissors were, and she wouldn't have had to ask Jennifer. If she hadn't had to do that, she might have gotten away with her plan. But she did have to ask. And so Jennifer must have wondered where Odessa had wandered off to with those scissors.

Oliver and Dad and Jennifer were doing a puzzle, a big one of underwater sea creatures. It looked as if it could take days to do, which was why Odessa figured she had some time to spare.

She pretended she was going to the room she shared

153

with Oliver, but when she saw no one was looking, she snuck into Dad and Jennifer's bedroom and closed the door. She found Jennifer's wedding dress hanging in the closet in a white zippered bag.

Odessa planned to quickly snip the straps with the scissors, but when she took the dress out and laid it on the floor she decided that maybe the straps weren't enough. What if Jennifer just pinned them?

She'd have to cut a hole in the middle. It wouldn't be easy: there was some sort of hard, underwire thing, and also, the fabric was so beautiful, so delicate, sewn with little tiny beads. She ran it through her fingers, feeling regret, *compunction*. But she'd made her brother a promise. Promises were precious too.

She grabbed hold of the scissors. She picked up the dress and searched for its middle.

Just then she heard Jennifer's voice.

"What is going on in here?" She was calm but mad. Yes, mad for sure. Jennifer was always so nice, so friendly: it was the first time Odessa had seen her mad. She looked like she'd maybe stopped breathing, but then she managed to shout out: "Glenn!"

Odessa could lie. Say she had no intention of ruining the dress, but there she sat with the scissors in one hand and the dress in the other. How could you not put two and two together?

Dad came running and froze in the doorway.

Odessa thought right then of a poem she'd loved when she was little about this kid who doesn't understand money and ends up giving away a dollar in exchange for five pennies. His dad's face turns red, and the kid thinks it's because his dad is proud, but of course he's not proud, he's angry. And when Odessa saw her father's red face she wondered if maybe he was the opposite of that dad in the poem—though he looked angry, maybe he was really proud.

Couldn't he see that she was trying to save her family? That it didn't matter about the dress, that what mattered was trying to do the right thing?

"Jennifer," he said. "Can you give me a minute alone with my daughter?" He reached out and pulled her into a hug. He was a head taller than Jennifer, and he kissed her curly hair. He let her slip slowly from his grasp and she left the room.

He turned to face Odessa and crossed his arms. She closed her eyes so she wouldn't have to see his reddening face. *Please, please, please be proud.*

He wasn't.

"Your dress yesterday," he said. "That wasn't an accident."

Like he'd been doing at the table, he was putting together the pieces of a puzzle. "And now this, Odessa. I hardly know what to say."

"Dad," she whispered.

"Quiet," he snapped. "I'm talking."

Dad never snapped. Odessa started to cry.

"This behavior is inexcusable. It's mean and hurtful.

You need to use your words, Odessa. I don't know how many times we have to tell you that. You need to talk when you're angry, not push or hit or act out like this." He gestured to the dress and the scissors on the floor.

"It's just . . . ," she said, choking back tears. "It's just . . ."

Dad came and sat next to her. His face had returned to normal Dad color. That was when Odessa found her words.

"It's just that you're supposed to love Mom."

"Oh, sweetie," he said, taking her chin in his hand and turning her to face him. "I do love Mom. I'll always love Mom."

"Then why are you remarrying Jennifer?"

"Because," he sighed. "Things change."

He said more, about two people growing apart, realizing you're different from who you once were, and blah, blah, blah.

Odessa was not listening.

She'd heard what she needed to hear. *I'll always love Mom.* When they talked about the divorce with Odessa and Oliver, her parents said things like *We still care about each other* and *We'll always be in each other's lives,* but this was the first time Odessa had heard him use the word *love.*

Words count. There are so many to choose from, and Dad had chosen *love.*

That was all that mattered.

And yes, things change. Odessa knew this better than anybody, because she had the power to change things.

Things change.

*

Before he drove her home, back to her attic, Odessa apologized to Dad. It was harder to know what to say to Jennifer.

She couldn't look her in the eye.

"It's not about you," Odessa said. "You're nice. You're always nice to me. You let me wear your lip gloss. And you gave me that dictionary with all the purple words. And your dress is so pretty."

Jennifer put a hand on Odessa's shoulder and squeezed. Odessa understood that squeeze: *It's okay.*

Still she added, "What can I do to make you feel better?" She wasn't just repeating what Mom had forced her to say when she upset Oliver. She really did want to make Jennifer feel better. She didn't want to hurt her.

Jennifer smiled. "You've already made me feel better."

Odessa wasn't sure she believed Jennifer, but it didn't matter. Soon enough that dress would be back hanging in the closet. The scissors would be back in the drawer. No one would stare at her with shock, or go red-faced with anger.

Unfortunately, it was too late to do anything about her lavender dress. She'd ruined it Saturday morning and she couldn't go back that far. She did so love that dress. But that was okay. She wasn't going to need it.

There would be no wedding between Dad and Jennifer. Odessa was going to change that too.

3 Hours

It was time for Odessa to admit that her GMOP needed an accomplice. Her GMOP was now a GMOOP—a Grand Master Oliver/Odessa Plan.

Plan to Go Back and Fix What Really Matters.

Plan to Re-Hyphenate the Family.

Plan to Get Our Old Life Back.

A plan this big required a coconspirator.

Though Uncle Milo was always her first choice when it came to a partner in crime, he was an adult, and he was Mom's brother. Odessa crossed him off her list.

It was time to fix things with Sofia.

Time to tell her everything.

Sofia was coming for a sleepover. They still talked on the phone all the time and played *Dreamonica* online, but it had been months since they'd had a sleepover. Time had almost erased Odessa's anger about the Theo haircut incident. It was funny how time could do that—change things without your even knowing.

Or it could have been that Odessa didn't care as much about what Sofia did or didn't say about Theo, because a miraculous thing had happened on Monday.

Theo asked her about math camp.

He asked *her*. Not Sadie Howell.

He told *her* his mom was signing him up, and he wondered if Odessa might want to sign up too, because, he said, applications were due at the end of the week.

Theo Summers. He asked if she wanted to go to math camp.

Math camp.

What a magnificent pair of words.

Mom had already signed her up for Camp Kattannoo, the same place she and Oliver went every summer—she had a collection of tie-dyed T-shirts and a drawerful of lanyards to show for it. Though she planned on getting her *old* life back, that didn't mean she couldn't go to a *new* summer camp.

Their conversation went like this:

THEO: Hey, what are you doing this summer?
ODESSA: (too embarrassed to say the word *Kattannoo* out loud) Going to camp. It's pretty cool. We design clothes and do weaving.

THEO: Oh. Sounds cool.

ODESSA: (Did she really just say "do weaving"?) It's okay, I guess.

THEO: Well, my mom signed me up for math camp. Applications are due by Friday.

ODESSA: Math camp?

THEO: Yeah. I thought maybe you might, you know, wanna go too.

ODESSA: Me?

THEO: (scratching his buzzed head) Yeah, you. You know, since you're like my math buddy, I thought you might want to go.

ODESSA: (cheeks in full Red-Light mode) Okay. I'll talk to my mom.

When she got home that afternoon, she wondered if the conversation had really happened. It seemed too good to be true. She'd always been told she had an "active imagination." Maybe it had run wild. Willy-nilly. Maybe she'd lost her marbles.

She wished she could go back and relive it, but she couldn't, because although it had happened at the end of the school day and she had the time, she only had three opportunities left to fix the Things That Really Mattered. It would be selfish to use an opportunity just to hear Theo say those words again, and she was no longer Odessa the Selfish.

So instead she inscribed the conversation into her journal, and while she did, she was able to decode the true meaning behind Theo's words:

Theo: Hey, what are you doing this summer?
(*What he meant:* I like you so much more than Sadie Howell.)
Theo: Oh. Sounds cool.
(*What he meant:* You are brilliant, just like me.)
Theo: Well, my mom signed me up for math camp. Applications are due by Friday.
(*What he meant:* I prefer girls with brown eyes.)
Theo: Yeah. I thought maybe you might, you know, wanna go too.
(*What he meant:* I can't face the summer without you.)
Theo: (scratching his buzzed head) Yeah, you. You know, since you're like my math buddy, I thought you might want to go.
(*What he meant:* I know we're only in fourth grade, but we'll be in fifth grade soon, so I think we should get married.)

Maybe it was this, the fact that Theo wanted to marry her, that made Sofia's comment those months back about his hair seem insignificant.

So she'd forgiven Sofia.

Odessa the Absolver.

*

Mom had ordered pizzas. There was talk of make-your-own-sundaes. It was shaping up to be a great sleepover.

Up in the attic, Odessa asked Sofia to swear herself to secrecy.

"Cross your fingers."

Sofia did.

"Now cross your toes."

Sofia removed her slippers. Four crossings were enough to gain Odessa's trust.

Odessa knew that most stories began at the beginning, so she started with the night she smashed Oliver's I Did It pottery. She told Sofia how she'd come downstairs to a plate of carrot cake. She told her about all the embarrassing things that had happened at school that Sofia didn't know about because Odessa had wiped them off the map. She told her about breaking into Mrs. Grisham's house. And Oliver's fall in the cafeteria.

Sofia hardly moved, hardly breathed. Her eyes barely blinked.

Odessa didn't tell her about the hundred-dollar bill, because she still felt a little guilty about it, just a little, and she didn't tell her what had happened with Theo and his haircut, because she figured there was no point in bringing up Sofia's less-than-perfect behavior when they were right in the middle of patching things up.

"So," Odessa said. "I realized this all must be for something. It has to have a purpose, right? And I don't want to go back to change the small things. I want to use these last opportunities to change what really matters. I want to get my old life back."

"Are you for real?" Sofia asked.

Odessa nodded.

Sofia made a face. She looked to Odessa, then to the attic floor, and back to Odessa again.

"Show me how this works," she said.

"I just roll up the carpet, close my eyes, and jump."

"That's all?"

"Yep."

"Show me."

"I can't," Odessa said. "I think there's only three times left and I have to make them count."

"Well," Sofia said, twirling a strand of blond hair on her finger, "if you want my help you have to show me how this works."

Odessa tried explaining again to Sofia why she didn't want to waste the opportunity when there wasn't something she needed to undo, but Sofia said, "Show me." She crossed her arms. "Or I'll tell."

"You'll *what?*"

"I'll tell. I'll tell your mom, or my mom, or somebody, everybody, about how you think you can turn back time by stomping on the floor." Sofia chuckled.

It wasn't a friendly sort of laugh.

Odessa couldn't believe her ears. Her ears that were

turning bright red with anger. She and Sofia were best friends. They had identical mansions and a dozen puppies, and they talked on the phone every day, and Odessa had hurt Claire terribly just to please Sofia, and they could communicate sometimes without using words.

Odessa tried this now. She looked at Sofia. She tried saying with her look: *Do you even know what you're doing? How you sound? What it means for our friendship? I'm asking you to catch me and you're stepping out of the way and letting me fall and split my head open.*

Sofia stared back. "Show me."

Odessa began to roll up the rug.

She stashed it next to her bookcase, made her way to the middle of the floor, and glared at Sofia.

"Hold on," Sofia said, scrambling to her feet and over to where Odessa stood. "I want to go with you."

"Why?"

"Because you're my best friend."

In a flash, Odessa played out two scenarios. In the first one she grabbed Sofia by the hand and they jumped together, back three hours to find themselves in their own homes preparing for their sleepover. She'd pick up the phone and call Sofia and listen to her marvel about the magic of time travel, and maybe even apologize for doubting her. Then she'd come over and they'd stay up all night whispering and plotting and putting the final touches on her GMOOP.

In the second scenario she'd shove Sofia out of the way and go back the three hours on her own, back to preparing for a sleepover at which she would not reveal the secrets of the attic.

Odessa chose option number two.

Despite what Dad had said, and Mom had said, and even Ms. Banville had said about how words rather than fists (or scissors) are the way out of conflict, Odessa gave Sofia a huge shove. Strong enough to knock her off her toe-crossing feet.

And then Odessa jumped.

Alone.

2 Hours

Odessa tried using words. If words really were the way out of conflict, then words should have helped her. Words should have been able to get her old life back.

But words weren't enough. Words were failing her. They didn't help with Sofia and they wouldn't help with Mom and Dad.

She couldn't just come out and tell Mom that Dad still loved her. Mom wouldn't believe her. And Dad wouldn't remember saying it, because Odessa had gone back and never asked for scissors, and she'd never taken the dress from the closet and Dad had never stared at her red-faced and disappointed. But Odessa knew. That was what mattered. And now all she had to do was confirm what she suspected: that Mom still loved Dad too.

She called another family meeting.

She couldn't just call a meeting to ask if they still loved each other, so instead she talked about math camp. She loved repeating her conversation with Theo—how *he'd* asked *her*. She'd told Mrs. Grisham and she'd told Uncle Milo and Meredith and she'd already told Mom and Dad and she'd even told Oliver, but still, she so enjoyed reliving it.

.Mom and Dad sat and stared.

"This is about math camp? Really?" They exchanged a look.

"You said we make all the big decisions together. As a family. Because we're still a family. Right?"

"Yes," Dad said. "We're still a family. But I'm not sure going to math camp qualifies as a big decision."

"It's big to me," Odessa offered lamely.

"Far be it from either of us to stand between our daughter and math. Of course you can go to math camp." Mom reached over and mussed Odessa's hair as if she were a child. Still, it was better than smelling her head. "Now hurry up and get out of here so you can have your dinner with your father and get home in time for bed."

It was a Wednesday. Dinner-with-Dad night.

"Why don't you come?" Odessa asked.

"Oh, no, honey." Mom didn't even look at Dad. "This isn't my night. This is Dad's night."

"Dad, you don't mind if she comes, do you?" Odessa

could feel Oliver's eyes on her. She could feel his wonder and awe.

Odessa the Brave.

"Um, well, no, I guess I don't mind."

What followed was an awkward exchange where Mom kept saying no, she couldn't, and Odessa kept saying of course she could, and Dad kept mumbling something about how it was okay by him, and then Odessa used the most powerful word she knew, the long, drawn-out *pleeeeeeeeeeeeeease?*

That was how they all wound up at Pizzicato for dinner together, the same place where Dad had told Odessa and Oliver that he was *re*marrying Jennifer, on the night before they moved into their new house with Mom.

But this night was the opposite of that night. This

night was *jovial*. They laughed and ate too much pizza and drank too much sparkling lemonade, and afterward as they walked back to Dad's car Odessa took each of her parents by the hand. If she hadn't been in the fourth grade and about to embark on a major relationship with a boy with buzzed hair, she might have jumped and let her parents swing her back and forth, back and forth, like she had when she was younger.

In the car Mom sat up front and Dad reached across her and took his minty tummy tablets from the glove compartment. Odessa inhaled their smell. Everything felt perfect. Once they reached home it would become clear that this was how it should always be, the four of them together.

But Dad dropped them off and drove away with a few short honks and a wave.

She'd have to do more.

*

The next weekend at Dad's, Odessa tried reminding him of all the ways Jennifer was not Mom. Jennifer was nice and pretty and she smelled good, but she belonged in someone else's family.

Mom belonged; Jennifer did not.

"Remember our family trip to Mexico?" Odessa put the emphasis on the word *family*.

"Of course," Dad said.

"That was the best."

And then:

"Remember that necklace you gave Mom for her birthday a few years ago?"

"Yes, I remember," Dad answered.

"That was one beautiful necklace." This time she put the emphasis on *beautiful*.

Odessa loved words. Even when you used the obvious ones, you could add so much meaning by just leaning on them a little.

But words had their limits. Dad reached over and gave Odessa's arm a squeeze. The squeeze was harder than the kind you give when you want to say I love you. This squeeze said: *Lay off the Mom stories in front of Jennifer.*

Nothing seemed to be working, but Odessa didn't lose faith. She knew what she had to do.

Stop the wedding.

She'd seen enough TV and movies to know that there was always a moment, an opportunity for someone in the audience to stand up and say: *I object!*

And this was what she'd have to do. She'd have to make Dad see, in that moment before he said vows he didn't really believe in, that he was remarrying the wrong person. She would stand up and she would grab her mother by the hand and she would shout: *I object!*

Or *I protest!*

Something like that.

The problem, however, was this: Mom wasn't invited

172

to the wedding, and Odessa's gesture was going to be a lot less grand without Mom there as a visual aid.

Odessa paced around her attic floor, squeezing the owl figurine in her fist. She talked to the boards as if they could listen.

Help me. You are here for a reason. I have this power for a reason. How can you help me stop this wedding? How can you help me realize my GMOOP?

Going back two hours couldn't change everything. It couldn't make Odessa live in her old house or make Mom and Dad still be married to each other or make Oliver less of a toad or make Odessa taller with pale blue eyes. It couldn't make Sofia trustworthy, or make Milo want to be with her more than with Meredith, or make Mrs. Grisham's husband still alive so she wouldn't be alone. And it couldn't make Mom appear at Dad's wedding so that Odessa could shout *I object!* and he'd see her and realize that he was making a big, fat mistake.

The attic could do none of that. She could only go back and fix something about her day that had gone in a way she didn't like.

And what she didn't like about the day that was rapidly approaching was that Dad was going to stand up and promise to love and cherish *Jennifer*.

She sat. And she thought. And she grabbed hold of her dictionary. And she thumbed through its fresh-smelling pages and all the purple words that couldn't help her. Jennifer had given her this dictionary. Jennifer was nice and thoughtful; someone else would want to marry her someday. Odessa felt *compunction*—she wanted Jennifer to be happy, she didn't want to ruin her wedding, her moment of triumph, but . . . Dad belonged to Mom.

She picked up her journal and a pen, but she couldn't get beyond the blank page. She stared at the phone, but there was nobody to call.

So she went to see Mrs. Grisham. Sofia was her best friend. Claire was her bus friend. Mrs. Grisham was her old friend.

It had been a while since she'd knocked on her door. Because Mrs. Grisham watched them after school, Odessa didn't have occasion to go to Mrs. Grisham's house, but this Sunday, one week before the wedding, that was what she did.

They sat together in the familiar parlor with the owl figurines.

Odessa stared at her shoes.

Mrs. Grisham let her stare. She didn't ask her what was wrong or why she was there or even if she wanted a cookie. She let her sit there silently, with all the eyes of those owls on her, while she figured out what she wanted to say.

"I don't know how to fix things."

Mrs. Grisham waited.

"I thought I could go back and fix things," Odessa continued. "That I could make changes, the kind of changes that matter, and I made a promise to my brother, and I have this power, this special power, and I kind of feel like you gave it to me, like you trusted me with the attic, you told me that I'd love living there, and I do love living there, but . . . I'm failing." Odessa's words got caught in her throat. "I can't change the big things. The Things That Really Matter," she croaked.

A long silence followed, during which Odessa swallowed back the tears that threatened to fall. She was in fourth grade. She wasn't a baby. She didn't want to cry.

"You've probably made more changes than you realize," Mrs. Grisham said.

"But I need to do more. It's not enough."

"So do more."

"But my powers . . . the attic, the magic, this power to go back . . ."

"Nonsense," said Mrs. Grisham. "Power comes from you. Not from magic."

"But I . . ."

"Nonsense."

Odessa wasn't used to Mrs. Grisham speaking to her this way. Rudely. Curtly. Dismissively. Plenty of adults spoke to kids this way—sometimes Sofia spoke to her this way—but never Mrs. Grisham.

Odessa went home deflated. She lay down on her bed and stared at the ceiling. She turned onto her side and caught sight of the door with no handle.

The crawl space.

She screwed up her courage, made her way to the opening, and climbed inside. Cobwebs brushed her face and tangled in her hair. There wasn't room to stand and jump, so Odessa squeezed her eyes tight, hugged her knees to her chest, and wished as hard as she could: *Take me to an alternate world. Pleeeeeeeease. I want to go someplace else. Somewhere different. I don't want to be here, where I can't change the things that matter.*

She sat like that, hunched over into herself, until the dust made her cough, her muscles ached, and she shook with cold.

Odessa felt the weight of her own failure all week long, and then, because time ticks forward, not backward, the morning of the wedding arrived.

Odessa woke in her attic to the ray of light shining in through her small dormer window. She walked over to her calendar with the cats on it and removed Saturday's cat to reveal Sunday's cat: a fat tabby in a black tuxedo and top hat.

Dad wasn't fat, and he wasn't wearing a top hat to the wedding, but still, the coincidence made her laugh.

She took out her new dress, light yellow and not nearly as twirly as the lavender one, and she laid it out on her bed. Then she looked at that bed and wished she could just crawl back into it and sleep until Monday. She couldn't. She knew that. But she *could* buy herself two more hours of sleep.

So why not?

The power to go back in time wasn't going to stop this wedding, but it could put it off just a little longer. And the bed looked so inviting. All week long she'd been sad. She was so, so tired.

Odessa went to the center of her room. She rolled up her cheetah-print rug. She closed her eyes, held her breath, and jumped, not knowing that she'd be racing right back to this same spot in a few short hours, using up her final opportunity, needing that final hour, to go back and change her future.

1 Hour

Odessa put on her dress and spun around. Then she spun harder. She got a little bit of twirl out of the edges of the pale yellow fabric, but still: disappointing. She went downstairs and knocked on Oliver's door. Mom stood next to him at the mirror, helping him with his pale yellow tie.

Odessa watched Oliver checking out his reflection. He looked the opposite of toadlike. Handsome, even. And Odessa could see from the way he stared at himself that he could see this too.

Mom was still wearing her bathrobe, but it was white, and Odessa could imagine her standing next to Dad in a white dress with delicately sewn beads and a wire thingy in the middle that made it hard to cut through. Mom could be the bride. Suddenly Mrs. Grisham's words came back to her.

Power comes from you, not from magic.

She couldn't give up. She had to get Mom to that wedding so that she could stand up and shout *I object!* and Dad could see he was making a big mistake.

"Mom, you need to get dressed."

"Why?" she asked. "I'm not going anywhere. Just to the movies with Milo and Meredith, but that's not until later."

"Just go put something nice on, will you?"

Mom looked at her and then at Oliver, and then she smiled, almost as if she understood.

"Well, you two do look dashing. I suppose I shouldn't just stand around here in my pajamas. I'll go get dressed and then we'll have a proper sit-down breakfast." She took in the sight of Odessa and Oliver in their matching outfits. "Me and my two gorgeous kids."

Odessa asked Oliver to set the table and he said he would, without sticking his tongue out or anything, and Odessa grabbed a piece of paper and a pencil and sat down to write a note.

Sometimes it was easier to get Mom to pay attention when she wrote down what she wanted to say.

Dear Mom,
I need you to come to the wedding with me so that Dad can see that he is making a big

mistake and so that I can say I object! and then we can go back to living together as a re-hyphenated family. Please. It is my SMOOP.

Love,

Odessa

She folded the note and then she folded it again. Her pale yellow dress had no pockets, so Odessa stuck it under her plate. She wanted it nearby when she gathered the courage it would take to hand it to her mother.

When she came back downstairs, Mom looked beautiful. Mostly, Mom looked tired, or frustrated, or just Mom-like. But this morning she wore a pretty flowered shirt, jeans, and boots with heels, and though that was a far cry from a white gown with tiny beads, it would have to do.

They sat and ate and talked as if it were just another morning, just another day, though of course they all knew it wasn't. Odessa mostly pushed her food around on her plate. She knew something that her mother and brother didn't. That today would be the day they'd begin their old life again.

Odessa pictured that calendar cat, the one in the tuxedo, standing with his paw around the waist of a cat in a flowered shirt, jeans, and boots with heels.

She smiled.

"Someone's happy," Mom said.

"Mom." Odessa felt her power, the power Mrs. Grisham said came from her, not from magic, rising up from her chest to her face, making her go warm, and probably red-cheeked too. "Mom, there's something I have to—"

Just then the doorbell rang.

Mom stood up. "I have a surprise."

Odessa and Oliver followed her to the front door. There stood a man in a black suit and a black cap. Behind him in the driveway was a long black stretch limousine.

Odessa could hardly believe it.

She'd always dreamed of riding in a limousine. In the pages of the tween magazines Mom didn't like her to read, the young stars of the shows Mom didn't like her to watch rode around in them. She'd asked, begged, cajoled for a ride in one.

Once, before their family trip to Mexico, she'd asked if they could take one to the airport.

Mom had said, "Isn't the fact that we're taking you on an airplane to another country enough for you?"

So Uncle Milo had driven them in his beat-up wagon.

And then she'd asked again on her ninth birthday for a ride in a limousine to anywhere: around town, Pizzicato, the Dairy Whip for an ice-cream cone.

But Mom had said, "No, that's absurd, you're nine years old."

If there was one thing Odessa could count on, it was Mom saying no to the things she wanted most of all.

"Your father sent the limo for you." Mom gestured to the man with the hat in his hands. "He'll take you to the church. Dad will meet you there."

One part of Odessa wanted to forget the note clutched in her palm and run to the limousine, climb in, blast some music, turn on the colored lights, pour herself some water in a champagne glass, and inhale the fancy polished leather.

"Cool," Oliver said. "This is so cool."

"Wait," Odessa barked. Oliver froze. "Mom," she said. "You have to come with us."

Mom laughed. Her eyes quickly welled with tears. "I can't go with you, honey. This is your father's wedding. It's his moment."

"But you need to."

Mom's tears made their way to her cheeks now, and Odessa knew that those weren't happy tears. Happy tears catch at your eyes. These trailed down her face.

"Here," Odessa said, and she handed her mother the note. It was one of the moments when words wouldn't have come anyway, so she was glad she'd written them down.

Mom unfolded the note and read it. She made a sound and then covered her mouth with her hand. The tears were sobs now, and even though Odessa never would have thought watching her mother cry like that could make her *jovial*, that was exactly what happened.

Mom loved Dad too.

That was why she sobbed like that.

"Come on, Mom," she said, and took her by the hand. "Let's get in the limo."

Mom wrapped Odessa in her arms. She buried her face in her scalp and took a deep whiff. Odessa tried to break free, but her mother's grip was fierce.

"You're a great kid," Mom whispered. "And I love you. And I want you to go get in that car and go to your father's wedding and I want you to have a good time. Do that for me, okay?"

"Not without you," Odessa said. "Mom. Please."

Mom shook her head no.

"Pleeeeeeeeeeease?"

Right then Odessa felt Oliver's not-so-small-anymore hand in hers. He gave her a tug.

"Let's go," he said. "It's gonna be okay."

Odessa looked at Oliver. She looked at Mom. She looked at the man with his hat in his hands who had taken several steps back from where they stood.

I can fix this, she thought. *I have the power.*

"Can I have your business card?" she called to the man.

"Excuse me?"

Mom chuckled. "He's legit, Odessa. Just get in the car."

"Please, sir," she said, using her politest voice. "May I have your business card?"

The man stepped toward her and reached into his inside jacket pocket. He pulled out a card with gold lettering and held it out. Odessa took it.

World-Class Limousines:
Let us take you for a ride you will never forget.
And at the bottom: the telephone number.

"Thanks!" she called over her shoulder as she ran from the entryway. What she didn't count on was Mom running after her.

"Come back here!" Mom shouted. "You can't run away from this."

As Odessa raced up the stairs she studied those numbers. She knew she couldn't take the card with her, so she needed to memorize them.

Luckily, Odessa was good with numbers.

She got to her attic a few steps ahead of Mom. She didn't bother with the rug. She didn't have the time, and anyway, what did the rug matter? The rug was a small thing. If she'd learned anything, it was that the small things didn't matter.

*

Odessa sat at the breakfast table in her pale yellow dress that didn't twirl. She had a pen in her hand and a blank piece of paper in front of her. She took the paper and balled it up and threw it in the trash.

She grabbed the phone in the kitchen and dialed the numbers still fresh in her mind.

"World-Class Limousines," a voice chirped.

"Yes, good morning." Odessa used the most adult voice

she could muster. "I'm sorry to tell you that we have to cancel an order. The car coming to One Twenty-One Orchard Street. Please refrain from sending it." She paused, not sure what else to say. "That is all."

"Will do," the voice said, and hung up. Odessa hadn't expected that to be so easy.

Oliver cocked his head. His look said, *What was that all about?* but Odessa just pretended she couldn't read looks.

Right then Mom came downstairs in her pretty flower shirt, jeans, and boots with heels. Again, Odessa thought she looked beautiful.

They sat and ate breakfast and the doorbell didn't ring.

Mom looked at her watch.

The doorbell still didn't ring.

Odessa cleared the dishes, careful not to spill anything on her pale yellow dress. She wanted to look her best when she shouted *I object!*

Mom was pacing now. She picked up the phone and hung it up again. She went to the front door, stepped outside, looked up and down the street, and came back in again.

"Oh boy," she said.

"What is it, Mother?" *Odessa the Innocent.*

"There seems to be a problem with your ride to the wedding."

"Why don't you just take us?"

"Because I shouldn't be the one to have to drive you. It's his responsibility to make sure you get there on time today of all days." Mom picked up the phone and dialed, held it to her ear, and then hung it up. "Voice mail. Typical."

She picked up the phone again. This time she called Uncle Milo. Uncle Milo, famous for doing nothing, had something he had to do that morning that prevented him from driving his niece and nephew to their father's wedding.

How Odessa loved Uncle Milo.

"Mom," Odessa said. "We have to go. We can't miss the wedding. Please. Time is running out."

As Mom went to get her keys, Odessa darted back up to the attic. She stood and looked around the room she loved so much, and she wondered if she'd be saying goodbye to it soon. With Mom and Dad getting back together, maybe they'd buy their old house again, or maybe get a new one.

She stood on her cheetah-print rug, the rug that hadn't been lost in the betwixt.

"Thank you," she whispered to the floor. "For everything."

She ran back downstairs, and they all piled into the station wagon that was not a limousine and sped off to the wedding Odessa was going to stop.

The streets she knew so well rushed by outside her window. Inside, her heart felt full to bursting.

Her new life was about to begin.

Or maybe it was that her old life was about to begin again.

Time can be tricky that way.

The New New House

Odessa sat down on a cardboard box marked *Odessa's stuffed animals.* She wasn't sure she was going to unpack this box. She wanted her new room to be grown-up. A fifth grader's room. Maybe she'd have Uncle Milo carry the box down to the basement for storage, since the new house had no attic.

This house was theirs. A forever house, Mom called it.

"Forever?" Odessa asked. Forever was a very long time, and time couldn't always be trusted.

Mom put a hand on her head and smiled. "Forever for now."

They'd bought it from a couple whose kids had grown up and gone off to college. There were someone else's scribbles on the kitchen wall and scuff marks on the stairs

189

from someone else's shoes, but Odessa didn't mind. They could paint the walls and refinish the wood. This was their *forever for now* house.

Odessa and Oliver wouldn't have to switch schools, but they would ride a new bus. She worried about Claire and their bus friendship, but then Claire said, "Why don't you come over after school sometime? We can hang out at my house."

So that was just what Odessa planned to do.

The new bus wouldn't take them by their old house, or their old old house. It traveled a new route that went by Dad and Jennifer's apartment, where it would pick up Odessa and Oliver every Thursday morning now that they'd turned dinner-with-Dad night into sleepover-at-Dad-and-Jennifer's night.

Dad and Jennifer's wedding had turned out differently from how Odessa had planned—obviously—because here they were, married to each other, four months later.

They were married, not *re*married.

When Odessa had arrived at the church that morning with only minutes to spare, Mom had pulled up to the entrance and kept the car running.

"Hurry up," she said. "You're late."

"You have to come," Odessa said. "Come inside with me."

"No, honey. You have to do this on your own. Not on your own," she corrected herself. "You have to do this with your brother. Your person in this world."

"Mom, please," Odessa pleaded. She wished she'd written that note. Wished she had a slip of paper that said what she needed to say, because it was hard to speak with the car running and the clock ticking.

"Please come inside so that I can shout *I object!* And Dad can see that to remarry means to do it again to the same person and then we can go back to our old lives and you won't have to go to work and Oliver will be happy and maybe we can move to a new house together but I still want my own room."

She held her mother's hand firmly, but she could feel Mom pulling away. Usually it happened the other way around—it was Odessa who tried to extract herself from a parental grip.

Mom took a deep breath and let it out again. Gathering up her courage, Odessa hoped, to walk inside the church.

"There are three things I want to say to you." Mom turned around in her seat completely, so that she faced Odessa and the struck-silent Oliver.

"One: I'm happy. I love my job and I love my kids and I'm starting to really like life the way it is. I love your father because he is the father of my children, but I do not want to be married to him anymore. I. Am. Happy."

She held up two fingers, the way the teachers at school did when they wanted to make sure the class was still paying attention.

"Two: It's okay for you to go in there and have a good

time. I don't want you to root against them out of some
sort of loyalty to me. Everything will be better if everyone
is happy. So let them have this day, and try to enjoy it too.
Weddings are fun and you're dressed to kill. And whether
you have a good time or not is entirely up to you."

"And three." She took her three fingers and reached
out to stroke first Oliver's and then Odessa's cheek. "I am
so proud of both of you. You are growing up so fast and so
beautifully."

Odessa noticed Oliver's hand in hers. She couldn't
have said who had taken whose hand first. He pulled her
toward the car door.

Words.

There would be no pushing or shoving or stomping or shouting *I object!* Mom had used her words. And they'd made Odessa see things differently, which, after all, is the purpose of words.

Odessa and Oliver got out of the car and stood in front of the church. Mom smiled and waved, gave a quick honk, and drove off.

*

Now, as Odessa unpacked her light yellow dress and hung it in her new closet, she thought about that day four months ago when Dad stood at the altar with Jennifer. He looked so tall and handsome. Her eyelids sparkled and her lips shimmered even more than usual. They held each other's hands and looked into each other's eyes and it was as if no one else was even in the church. When the minister asked if anyone had any objections, Odessa knew she couldn't object to Dad and Jennifer, she'd just have to get used to Dad and Jennifer, and maybe that wouldn't be so hard.

Later she danced with Dad, and she danced with Jennifer, and even Oliver danced like those hamsters in the commercial he loved, and what she'd thought would be the worst day of her life turned out to be lots of fun, just like Mom said.

Odessa returned home that night after Dad and

Jennifer left for their honeymoon, and she went to her attic. She rolled up her rug, closed her eyes tight, and jumped, not because she wanted to undo anything about that day—the day was sort of wonderful—but because she wanted to see what would happen.

Was she really out of opportunities to make a change? To undo something about her day that had gone in a way she didn't particularly like?

She jumped and she jumped harder, pounding her feet against the floor until her mother finally came upstairs and asked, "What is this racket all about?"

"Nothing, Mom," Odessa said. "It's all over now."

*

Odessa took a look around her new room. There were more boxes to unpack than she remembered packing. She pulled out her certificate from math camp and hung it over her desk. She and Theo weren't in the same group, but they shot baskets together during free time and sometimes ate lunch together. The math was hard but not too hard, and she'd made friends with a girl who didn't go to their school, a summer friend, and Theo had started growing his hair shaggy again.

She could hear Oliver in his room next door. He was singing a song from Camp Kattannoo. He'd made friends there. Friends who were not furry and small and smelly. He was doing okay without her and her GMOP or GMOOP. He was looking forward to the third grade.

She'd given him a housewarming gift. A huge pirate Lego set he'd had his eye on for months.

"Wow! This thing costs like a hundred dollars!"

Odessa knew exactly how much it cost.

She heard a knock on her door. She figured it was Oliver, because she'd reminded him all through the move about knocking and privacy and not listening in on her phone calls.

Or maybe it was Sofia, who'd said she wanted to stop by to check out Odessa's new room, and Odessa had said *Come on over* because she still loved Sofia. Sometimes Sofia wasn't the world's greatest best friend, but other times she was.

She opened the door.

It was Mrs. Grisham.

Even though it had only been a day since she'd seen her, and even though she'd never done it before, Odessa gave her a big hug.

"You left this behind," Mrs. Grisham said, reaching into her pocket and pulling out the small glass owl. "I found it in your attic."

"It's not my attic anymore."

"No, I suppose it's not." She stared into Odessa's eyes. "But it was for a time."

Mrs. Grisham stepped inside and took a look around

195

Odessa's new room. She walked to the center of it and stood. She tapped her foot on the floor.

Like Odessa hadn't already tried that!

There was nothing at all magical about this new room, and that was perfectly fine by Odessa.

"You're going to love it here," Mrs. Grisham said, just as she had that first time she showed Odessa the attic house, although now Odessa knew that her bark wasn't an order, it was just the voice of someone who has lived a long time and knows certain things.

"I think I will," Odessa said. "I think I'm going to love it here."

She took the owl from the old woman's hand and she put it on her desk.

Her desk. Her room.

Her home.

Forever, for now.

About the Author

DANA REINHARDT lives in San Francisco with her husband and their two daughters. She is the author of *A Brief Chapter in My Impossible Life*, *Harmless*, *How to Build a House*, *The Things a Brother Knows*, and *The Summer I Learned to Fly*. Visit her at danareinhardt.net.